The Ground

Never Sleeps

CHAPTER ONE

The storm drew its strength from the monstrous dark sea, absorbing its power and driving the rain hard into the land, where it hit like sharp needles against Michael's face. He gazed into the distance from the clifftop on which he stood, creating shapes in his mind from the massed dark clouds that rolled across the sky, stalking the coastline. Like a leviathan of the sky gods, once prayed to, from an age long since passed to the buried annals of time. There was an ominous presence to the shapes; a manifestation of a darkness from within his mind. The visceral roar of the crashing waves at the base of the cliff drew Michael closer to the edge.

The hour was late and the storm grew heavier; the depth of the darkness was all-consuming. Michael hunkered down into his coat, pulling the collar tight around his neck, the cold rain threatening to penetrate his body. He resisted his instinct to retreat from the harshness of the weather; he liked the storm and the feeling of the bitter cold rain and the sound it made when it hit his wax coat. He had been at this spot many times before. Away from the world with only his thoughts and a sense of existence which he only got from being so close to the edge of the cliff. He gambled with chance on the precarious edge. He looked into the absorbing void that was the two-hundred-and-fifty-foot drop to the waves, which were so very inviting. This place had become his own sanctuary from life and the pain from living in it. It was time to leave. The surge of adrenaline of nearly ending all that he was had been sufficient; he could return and stay in this world a little longer.

Michael left his sanctuary by means of a little-used gravelled track that wound down towards a small grassed car park. The moment he felt his keys inside his coat pocket the pain of life was on the attack and, just like the waves hitting the cliff, so too was reality. Reality often hurt. It ate at his insides. He looked at his car, which through the passing of time was now considered a classic, the red colour still distinguishable from what little light the moon gave through the rain that was running off the body of this romantically beautiful machine. Michael slumped into the driver's seat, grabbed the wheel with both hands and contemplated the consuming thoughts of his depression. It had been something he had always suffered from since a young age. He had now got what he wanted, what he had worked so hard for, so why could he not shift these dark clouds that continued to haunt him?

The thought evaporated as the ignition sparked the engine to life and brought Michael back from his dark reverie. He slipped into first gear and gently rolled away, picking up speed as the car found its way onto the solid black ground that was the narrow coastal lane back home.

The car gently purred its way through the gated stone arch and crept up the gravel drive, Michael allowing it to come to a restful stop. Opening the large oak door, Michael walked through to the only remaining medieval part of his ancient home: the archaic hall with a small arched doorway at the opposite end which led to an adjacent room which was newer by a couple of centuries or so. It contained a magnificent edifice of a fireplace where his faithful companion lay sound asleep waiting for his master's return. Michael took off his wax coat and hung it upon an iron hook and kicked his boots to the base of the wainscoting. Somewhat delayed in its responses, the animal awoke and with an awkward stagger rose to its feet and entered the hall. Upon seeing his master's figure through his greying eyes, the dog immediately perked up and launched himself with the enthusiasm of a child on Christmas day towards the misty outline. Michael smiled as he greeted his faithful companion; his home was indeed in safe hands.

The weather outside had not abated as the storm travelled inwards, conquering the land. The early hours past midnight took over from the day as Michael sat contentedly in his leather chair, swirling his favoured whisky. A sentimental drink from when as a young lad he would watch his father open a bottle with reverence after a hard day's work. A warm, pulsating glow came from the fire, every crackle giving a feeling of friendship, repelling the sense of loneliness that sometimes came with living alone. The dog now lay at his feet enjoying the warmth and security and the knowledge that his master was home safe. The two had been in each other's life for the last fourteen years; an Australian Cattle Dog exhibiting a personality and cunning that any fairy-tale fox would be proud to own. The view from the chair looked out onto the gravel drive; his car was a black silhouette against the first glow of the emerging day, and just as shapes appeared in the clouds, Michael now saw shapes in the dark as his eyelids drooped, bringing on sleep.

The sharp ringing of the house telephone brought Michael grudgingly out of his slumber. Making his way to answer it, he looked at the clock in the hall. Four o'clock – still early morning.

A voice spoke almost furtively. "Michael… it's Sarah."

"Sarah!? It's four in the —"

"Michael… you need to come home, can you come home please?"

Somewhat vexed and still adjusting his senses to the early-morning call, Michael barked a gruff response. "What's wrong?"

"I need you to come." Sarah's lips sounded as though they were pressed against the mouthpiece. "I've seen someone, or something, in the grounds. I'm scared."

There was an anxiety in Sarah's voice that Michael hadn't noticed before.

"Okay, I'm sure it's —" Michael's attempt at reassurance was cut short.

"Michael, I've seen them more than once. We're here alone… something… someone… I think someone has been here tonight," she stammered.

"Well, have you phoned the police?" he asked, trying to gather coherent speech.

"Yes! Of course I have! They've been before but couldn't see any evidence; they say they can't do anything but will send a patrol car if they have one free." She sounded irritated and alone.

"Okay, I'll get my things together and I'll head up," he said, though not without betraying some annoyance at the inconvenience.

"Thank you, it's good to hear your voice."

With that the tone went dead, leaving Michael alone again. What or whom could she have seen? His thoughts were still fairly incoherent, though, such had been the depth of his slumber.

"Flint!" he shouted. "Come here, boy. Let's get you some early-morning breakfast."

His faithful companion snapped to attention and attacked his food as if he'd never been fed before. Michael leapt upstairs, missing every other step as he went. Turning the light on in the master bedroom, he gave an amused sigh at the energy-saving light bulb, which seemed to wait until you left the room before fully illuminating the surroundings. That's how they save energy, he thought to himself: you give up ever turning them on in the first place. Pulling a small holdall from on top of the wardrobe, he quickly packed a few essentials for what he felt would just be a reassurance mission; the trip would probably be longer than the stay.

"Flint! Come here, boy. Let's say goodbye for now, mate. I'll be back home soon. Mary will look after you."

Mary was almost as faithful to Michael as Flint. A lady of age, who had lived in her house most of her life, just a short walk down the lane. No one alive now knew who had lived there before. She adored Michael as if he was one of her own, never forgetting the time he had rescued her cat one stormy night from a flash flood. The storm had caused severe damage to the remnants of a medieval church, which had been rendered a shadow of its former self.

There was a chill to the air, Michael noticed, as he threw his holdall onto the passenger seat of his car. Wouldn't be long before the snow paid a visit, he thought to himself. The rain was turning to a gentle drizzle as he drove through the arch and out onto the road, stopping off at Mary's house to post a hastily scribbled note asking her to look after Flint. Good old girl, he thought, pausing pensively. He really must make sure he got her a worthy Christmas present this year. He dashed back down the path and got back into his car, a foggy glaze already misting the windscreen. As the car gripped the gravel verge it spun up the loose stone, which hit the inside of the wheel arch with a rattle.

The drive back to his family home was going to take some time, mostly on A roads and winding country lanes. Michael had a love–hate relationship with motorways. They were okay when flowing but you could quickly come unstuck and lose a whole day in stopped traffic, not something he could risk on this journey.

Even so, it was now mid-afternoon and Michael had been on the road for longer than he cared to be. The drizzle had now turned into a storm which continued unabated. Roadworks, obscure diversions and the morning traffic had all helped to slow his progress, and adding to his frustration now was the lack of signal on his phone.

Suddenly the car lurched away from his control, the steering wheel slipping from his grasp as a loud bang came from one of the tyres. He grabbed the wheel with both hands as he tried to gain control, but to no avail. The car collided violently with an obscured tree stump at the roadside. "BLOODY HELL!" he shouted as the car skidded sideways along the road, regaining partial control just in time to aim it towards an open gate into a field. With tightly gripped hands he kept hold of the wheel. Michael was panting with subsiding panic, sweat creating beads on his forehead. He slumped into his seat, his heart in his throat, the adrenaline dissipating.

"Shit," he muttered.

Getting out of the car, he found the ground was sodden. He took a look at whatever damage had been done and to inspect the blowout. One tyre was in shreds and part of the side panel had been damaged. The car looked a sorry state sunk into the mud. Standing by the car he surveyed the sky; rain still poured down.

With no signal on his phone, Michael started walking; a short distance, as it turned out, down the lane, to his relief finding a local garage. The storm seemed to be moving away in his opposite direction and although he usually liked the harsh weather, on this occasion he appreciated the relief.

The establishment was the kind you rarely find now. A building that dated from the 1930's with very few, if any changes since that time, double wooden doors pinned back to the brickwork partly obscuring a Dunlop tyre advertisement. The place appeared deserted at first until a portly figure sprang up from behind the open bonnet of an evidently loved Rover P5, wearing what looked to be a blue boiler suit, though the colour was indistinguishable from the thick layer of oil and grease that seemed to encompass the whole of his body.

"'Ello, sir."

"Hello," Michael replied. "I've had an accident just up the road. Tyre blew out on me and sent me flying into a field. Lucky no one else was around!"

"I see," said the stout fellow, who was now cradling an oily rag in a polite attempt to clean his hands. "You'll need help getting that out. I'll send young Tom up with you and get it back 'ere. That okay, sir?"

With a grateful smile of acknowledgement, Michael replied, "That's blinding, thank you."

He hadn't envisaged such a direct response to his plight, expecting a nonchalant rebuff at the complexity of recovering his car, the garage owner offering his mate's costly rescue service or enquiring if he had breakdown cover, which Michael did not! He looked down at his phone: still no signal. "Do you mind if I use your phone?" he asked.

"Of course, just through there, on the counter."

The phone kept ringing; he tried twice, letting each time play out, but still no answer. Michael wanted to let his sister know not to worry, he was on his way. He would have preferred an answer to his call, relieving some of his own anxiety, but she could easily have been doing any number of things that meant she couldn't answer, or so he reassured himself.

By the time the tractor had pulled his car from the muddy field and got it back to the workshop, two hours had passed. Parts and labour wouldn't see the car fit for the road until at least the weekend, he guessed. The garage owner reassured Michael that he would treat it as a priority job and offered directions to a hamlet where he was more than likely to get a room for the duration of the repair should he wish to stay local. Buses were infrequent and trains were worse still. Michael decided it was just as easy to stay. He was hungry, his body ached for food and it was getting late in the day now. He hadn't been aiming to stay anywhere, he was planning on driving through the night, but events had now conspired against him.

The quaint little B&B resembled the lid of a gift-shop biscuit tins. The proprietor, an old lady who looked far too frail for the job, showed unexpected vitality and warmth in her smile as she handed him the keys.

"Hope you don't mind the odd resident ghost. You tend to get them in a building as old as this. Oh, and we do a light meal of an evening if you would like me to put you down for that?"

"Yes please, and as long as the ghosts don't steal a good night's sleep," Michael said, chuckling back. He felt embarrassed by his muddy appearance and hoped the proprietor wouldn't think less of him for it.

He climbed the deep, snug, crimson-carpeted staircase, which had an old ship's rope running through loops fastened to the wall as a stair rail. Each step brought a subtle groan from the ageing timbers of the staircase. At the top there was a narrow landing. No door looked the same in size and the one to his room had a slanted top to it. The room was small with a sash window. His holdall of clothes looked woefully inadequate as he unpacked. He scanned the room for the kettle and the complementary tea and coffee. It was always something Michael looked forward to whenever he stayed away from home. He couldn't explain the simple pleasure it brought and a brew was the first task to be done; there was nothing quite like it. One time when there were no such facilities it had marred the entire weekend for him, and he never paid a return visit. This time the tray was soon located in a nook by the window. After the quickest of showers, he went down to the dining room where an abundance of doilies lay on the tables, and damask cushions sat plumped on two large sofas at either end of the room.

"Hello, dear."

The elderly proprietor appeared through a doorway. Behind her, Michael could see a glimpse of an adjoining room that had the promise of a comfortable rest with a coffee before bed.

"Now… a man of your stature must be ready to eat a horse," she said.

"I certainly am," Michael replied, scanning the menu with salivating excitement (all food at all times was salivating to Michael).

"Soup of the day sounds good, followed by the house burger, no sauce, thank you."

After dinner, Michael relaxed in one of the leather chairs in the adjacent lounge, wishing Flint could be there to enjoy the fire with him. The purpose of the journey had almost faded when he looked at his phone. Finally, a signal! The first call was to his sister, and again he waited for her to answer, his thoughts filled with the home that he was trying to get back to. Still no answer came and he gave up on the second attempt, putting any concerns to the back of his mind. The next call was to Mary. This time the waiting brought no anxiety but rather a warm feeling as a soft voice, only slightly diminished by the years, answered, "Hello."

"Mary! It's Michael, how are you, okay to talk? You're not busy?" he said with an almost apologetic undertone.

"Oh, hello, dear. I got your note. Is everything okay?"

"Yes, I'm sure it will all be fine. I've had to stop over en route in a B&B; had trouble with the car. How's Flint?"

"Oh, he's just fine, dear. Hope you don't mind but I've brought him down 'ere with me, bit easier I thought; still keeping one eye on the house. He's a joy to have," answered Mary.

The call lasted not much more than five minutes but left Michael satisfied that at least all was well at home. He stared into the fire and thought of his sister again. There was still no answer to his call. Any anxiety that may have intruded into his mind was pushed away, and Michael retired to bed, made another cup of coffee and settled in. He had never suffered from too much coffee… at least he didn't think so. He was the only person he knew who felt coffee made him sleep better.

The morning sun shone through the net curtains. Michael lay perfectly still in bed. His eyes gazed around the room, bringing himself to his senses. He didn't often have such deep sleeps, being more of a light sleeper, always perturbed by his thoughts when trying to get off. The bed was heaven. He felt as if it had swallowed him whole in the night in a warm embrace. He clicked the switch to the kettle, set out his cup for coffee and relaxed under a nice warm shower, the hot water soothing his body. Coffee made, he savoured the moment in silence, looking out of the window. Once there was no more coffee left in the pot he got dressed and went down for breakfast.

"How was your night?" the old lady asked, as she poured a second helping of fresh orange juice.

"Lovely, thank you, very peaceful."

After breakfast Michael went for a walk to be with his thoughts. Thoughts, good or bad, didn't always come; like a lot of men Michael had an extraordinary ability to operate in a kind of energy-saving mode and quite happily think of nothing at all; not a single thought would pass between his synapses and he'd be content. His thoughts more often than not would come at night. In the here and now, though, he could appreciate the beautiful surroundings. The signal to his phone had gone again, all the more frustrating as losing signal was a rarity these days. Gone were the times you had to hold your hand high, walk around seeking a connection, and find that invariably it would go again when you seized your chance and held it to your ear. Michael was feeling somewhat impotent staying in a cosy B&B and wanted to make contact with his sister; he could try the phone where he was staying, he thought. The track he was walking on was enclosed with trees on both sides, branches bent over, limiting the sunlight. It took him on a downward slope crossing a brook and up a slight gradient to an open field with a few cows at the far end. He continued along the footpath, enjoying the feeling of being close to nature and the fresh smell of the earth as he entered a copse which divided the field in two. Through the other side he jumped down into an old ha-ha, long disused, with remains of a stone wall that had crumbled into smaller sections of its once larger self.

Back in his room, Michael was about to go and ask if he could use the proprietor's phone when he took one last look and found he had the slightest of signals… and a hushed voice answered.

"Hello."

"Hello?" Michael replied.

"Oh Michael, where are you?" It was Sarah.

"I've had a bit of trouble with the car and have had to get it repaired… old classics, that's the trouble, takes more time. I've been trying to call you but I've had a poxy signal and when I have managed to get through you haven't answered. I'm not going to get to you till the weekend by looks of it."

"You're okay though?" asked Sarah, concern in her voice.

"I'm okay, so…what's going on? And where have you been?"

"There's been something going on here, I don't want Dad to know so I'm trying to keep my voice down. Something is here; I think… I think it's stalking us."

There was a pause.

"My nerves feel at breaking point."

It was becoming obvious to Michael things were more serious than he'd thought. Sarah had taken a break from work to look after their father, after he had suffered a stroke. Their mother had died five years before. There had always been stories about the old house and its winding passageways, but none he'd taken seriously. The house was a beautiful relic. Both Sarah and Michael had been lucky enough to grow up there after their mother and father bought it with hopes to restore it to its former glory. It had been a labour of love, the finances always stretched, with some parts still needing to be done though on a whole the work was complete.

"On that night I had left Dad by the open fire in the study and was in the old servants quarters. I was looking out of the window, just looking through my own reflection into the night. I was daydreaming really. But then I realised I had stopped daydreaming and could see something, someone… I realised it was something in the shape of someone. And before you start I know the difference in what I was looking at. It was out there in the darkness but I could feel it with me, touching my very senses with darkness. I felt a perverse security in fixing my gaze on the thing and not looking to see if my senses were lying. It moved, but not by any means that made sense. It was hooded and I felt certain it had noticed me. To it, there was probably no window in the way, no defence, no discernible way that I could be safe; I may as well have been in a field all alone, surrounded by the night, vulnerable to its intentions. I grew colder, so cold. I closed my eyes before quickly opening them and it was suddenly there at the window staring straight through me. The fear I felt was overwhelming. I fell to the floor, from the shock more than anything. But the horror, Michael, the sheer horror. I felt dread fill my body. The stench of death…" The emotion of retelling the event had clearly got the better of her.

Michael was hesitant to reassure his sister with an offer of an explanation; he didn't quite know what to make of it himself. Perhaps she had seen something, but he didn't betray his personal thoughts that someone was playing silly beggars, or worse. But he needed to leave the B&B as soon as possible.

Michael went back to the garage. There were numerous cars in various states of repair that he hadn't really noticed on his first visit. Two in particular were slumped in the corner with visible signs of having been there for some time. A bird had made its home inside one of the cars' wheel arches, and it was sitting on the twisted remnants of the braking mechanism.

"Hello, young sir!" announced the garage owner.

He appeared from behind the workshop door, welding mask in one hand and a freshly filled tobacco pipe in the other. Michael wondered how this man had avoided setting himself alight – the boiler suit soaked in petrol and oil was enough of an ignition risk in itself.

"I take it you've come to see how your car is getting on? Well, it's all ready!" stated the portly man triumphantly.

"Fantastic news." The relief in Michael's voice was evident. Now he could get back on track. He was feeling a sense of urgency since the phone call.

"Thought you'd appreciate that," said the mechanic with a subtle wink in his eye, placing the pipe back in his mouth and sending up plumes of smoke. Putting the welding mask to one side, he made his way to the front of the garage.

"It's just round the corner here. I'll get your keys and I'll have the invoice ready… won't be a tick."

Michael followed him and there was his car, ready, valeted, and of course with fully inflated tyres. It felt as if a limb had been saved by a miracle after a doctor had diagnosed amputation. The short drive back to the B&B felt fantastic and the tip he'd left was well worth the extra, Michael surmised. He couldn't wait to get packed and en route again. He waited at the front desk to pay his final bill and say his fond farewells.

"Hope you had a pleasant stay. Everything to your liking?" the proprietor inquired.

"Yes, thank you, very warm and cosy."

"Oh good; no interruption from our resident ghosts then?" she asked with a somewhat loaded and interrogatory look on her face.

With a confident chuckle Michael replied, "No, and besides that sort of thing doesn't bother me. If I were to ever be wakened by one, I should think I'd just let them go about their business while I got back to my slumber."

"Well, safe journey," she said with a soft tone.

Back on the road, Michael was eager to catch up on lost time. As the car tyres gripped the country lanes, he thought about his sister. He started to work the gears harder, putting real determination into each bend of the road, pushing and willing the car to propel itself forward from each turn. The day was getting on. Snow-filled clouds that had hung in the air were now letting loose a flurry of white that was blanketing the hedgerows and distant copses in the surrounding fields, giving an ancient feel to the earth. The glowing of the car's headlamps through the haze of snow gave what little light there was in the impinging grip of the blizzard, isolated on cold country lanes.

But he was damned if he was stopping again, choosing instead to drive on!

CHAPTER TWO

It stood there as if risen from out of the snow-covered ground. An edifice of an unmistakably old grandeur. This ageing relic of the past no doubt would have once hosted a cacophony of parties, invited the top echelons of society and employed a workforce large enough to give any modern small business a GDPR headache. It was a machine built to impress a people in an age now gone. Yet still it stood there. A being of age. One that had seen loss and happiness with the changing world, a ghost from a past time that had long since ceased to exist.

Michael was back at the family home. The large, opaque door was cloven in two, with one side fixed, bolted shut. The other side was already ajar. Michael pushed it open to enter a large enclosed porch with a Georgian lantern hanging from its vaulted ceiling. The doors in front of him were, in contrast, more gentle, with mullioned windows. Unlocked. Michael entered the grand hall that housed an even grander chandelier and an elegant staircase that rose above him to the upper floors. Two doors either side of him led into different rooms, with a further doorway at the end of the hallway, sheltered by the staircase. He called Sarah's name but there was no answer. He stood still. He thought he had just heard someone, almost a faint giggle, he thought. It didn't come again; silence held the ground. It was nothing; he chose not to question what his imagination had quickly conjured in the empty, silent space. He hadn't actually been back home for a long time, so somehow the place felt unfamiliar to him yet with a sense of belonging at the same time. The grandfather clock had continued its duty; standing forthright, ticking heavily as Michael crossed the hallway. He called out for his sister again. His father this time… nothing. Nothing didn't need to mean anything, it was a large house with expansive grounds. No need to worry, not yet at least. His nerves made him feel as though he was being watched, judged, perhaps even stalked by something that had yet to decide what to do with him. He was beginning to get annoyed. If his sister was out in the grounds that meant she'd left the house unlocked; anybody could help themselves. She's her own worst enemy, he thought.

Walking around the rear of the house on the gravelled path, he surveyed the stone patio that reached out to terminate at the sprawling lawns with two great pillars, each holding an Atlas's globe. Stone steps drew your gaze into the grounds and woodlands beyond. He suddenly had a glimpse into his past, remembering playing there as a child with his toys. This past seemed so distant now, somehow uniquely old to him. He looked through each window to see into rooms with no one present. Turning the corner of the great building he saw two patio doors hooked back against the stone wall and his sister sitting at a small bistro table under an umbrella with their father beside her in his wheelchair. A pot of tea and a Chemex coffee pot sat in front of her.

He called to her. "Sarah!"

Sarah gave a startled jolt as she turned. "Michael!" She got up and gave him a big hug. "Oh, thank God you're here. Come and take a seat, say hello to Dad; he's doing so much better, some words are coming back."

Michael really wanted to deal with the unlocked door and admonish her over the lack of security but thought better of it and cheerfully greeted his father. "Alright, Dad, how ya doing? Good to see you."

With a gentle nod and a murmur giving way to a modest smile the old man stroked his son's arm in grateful acknowledgement. Michael sat down and poured the coffee, trying to ignore the embarrassment he felt from the guilt of not having visited much sooner.

Out of earshot from his father he leant over to Sarah. "So… what's with sitting outside in this weather? It gets any worse you'll be a couple of odd-looking snowmen"

Sarah replied with a furtive furrow in her brow. "It seems distant now, as if it's a hazy memory or an unwanted nightmare that you try and forget. But I'm left feeling so nervous, I've felt desperate sometimes. If I'm being honest I think the first time I saw something was a while back."

Sarah told Michael of a figure in the woods that seemed to disappear when she tried to focus on who or what it might be. She'd not really connected it to later events until now. The figures became more and more frequent, then the noises started in the house; telling him this made her shiver, as though she hadn't admitted to herself or managed to dispel her fears at feeling out of control. Some rooms were fine when you entered them, yet other parts of the house seemed uninviting, didn't feel like home any more. Sometimes it would feel as if someone was being interrupted in their task when you walked into a room.

"When I'm out here, I feel safe; well, sometimes. Today has been one of those days, when the house in some way feels threatening. As if someone is always in the room with you. It's horrible, Michael. I suppose you think I'm talking nonsense; its fine, I can see it in your face," she added, giving him a get-out clause.

"Well," Michael replied, not wanting to give any signal of how he'd felt when he entered the hallway. "That's something alright, and I'm not sure what to say, but I'm here now, so let's get inside. I'll have a proper scope of the house. You sort the fire out and get Dad comfortable and we'll settle in with a nice bit of nosh! How's that sound?"

"Yeah, that sounds good. I feel better already now you're here." Sarah smiled, and as she said this she glanced upwards to one of the bedroom windows, almost as if daring herself to see something.

Perhaps to give herself permission not to go back inside if she were to see something. Nothing was there, but it certainly didn't feel that way. The window revealed no figure but the room somehow didn't look empty either.

There was silence as Michael defensively stalked the rooms, having left his sister and father in the sitting room. All this bloody way and buggering up the car for this, he thought. Downstairs was easy enough; the rooms were large, built to impress. There were two enclosed corridors on the ground floor that once served as the staff passageways. So the servants could not be seen, heard or – heaven forbid – accidentally engaged in an awkward glance from the master of the house. The household staff of days gone by could go about their masters' bidding without anyone needing to notice them, or indeed even pay much care to their eventual demise. Names were rarely important; lives often mattered even less.

Upstairs the lack of natural light gave an unwelcome feeling, especially in the current situation. Michael recalled that faint giggle he thought he'd heard earlier, then quickly ushered the thought away; he didn't want to entertain any ghostly thoughts while negotiating the upper corridors. Michael stopped in one of the bedrooms and took a moment to gaze out of the window. The ledge was wet from the condensation on the glass. Michael would have been seen looking out by anyone who might have been coming up the drive. However, unlike Michael, who thought he was alone, what they would have seen was two figures gazing out form that bedroom window. One clear, one dark. Michael felt an involuntary shiver and left the room to carry on with his search. He went methodically room to room, to confirm to his own satisfaction the answer to a question he surmised he may need to ask later… were they alone in the house? Investigating the upper floor and its rooms to complete his search, he turned around suddenly, convinced he had just been touched. The sense of unknowing had brought on watery eyes and he stood quite still. Alone. A little afraid, too. Silence. Focused on the empty space in front of him that a second ago was at his back, he was aware of the emptiness. His mind searched for a rational thought, a way out of his frozen state. There was nothing there, just his imagination… that was all! His mind playing tricks on him, preying on the situation. He felt certain, convincing himself of this truth.

The final floor was cold, the heating having been turned off in this part of the house for some time. Narrow corridors that navigated the roof space, permitting entry to the adjacent rooms. Michael did not like it up here. His imagination was trying to assert itself, even more so now. Most of the rooms had been modestly decorated and used for display cabinets housing hobbies and personal treasures. Some just for storage. There were a few rooms that still had the Victorian décor and the servants' meagre furniture remained. Bedstead, knob-handled chest of drawers and built-in cupboards that at some point in their life had had wallpaper lining the shelves inside. These rooms were musty and smelt old. The green lead paint could still be seen in places. Michael skittered about and rapidly left, sufficiently satisfied that no one was there. He was glad to be back on the ground floor again; the upper rooms felt isolated and cold. Sarah was in one of the armchairs, the fire roaring, its crackling giving a primordial sense of security and defence. It was a friend, a close companion for the night.

"All good," he said, and sat down by the fire, eyeing the drinks cabinet. "House all locked up down here?"

"Yes, it's all secure for the night, and thank you for checking upstairs. Don't think I'm brave enough. What shall we have to eat?"

"I'll put something together," he replied, beginning to feel the effects of the drive as parts of his body started to hurt as they sometimes do when you're so tired.

A small feast had soon been consumed, the kitchen showing the unmistakable effects of Michael's cooking. All three felt safe in each other's company. The room was aglow with warmth and reminiscence. Outside, the flurry of snow had turned into a steady fall, disguising the landscape so that nothing remained recognisable; even Michael's car had vanished under a white blanket. Their father had nodded off, gently snoring into his slumber. Sarah too was feeling sleepy, less anxious now and secure enough to just close her eyes. Michael stared into the fire, hypnotised by the degradation of the burning wood. Other than this one room the house lay in darkness, and all was quiet. The only sound to break this stillness was the movement of the hands of the grandfather clock in the hall. The only witness to what might stalk the family that night. It had borne witness many times.

All three had fallen asleep and the fire began its slow decline into oblivion. The warmth of the room slowly retreated from the walls, encompassing just the inner circle of the three of them. It was two in the morning when Michael woke; Sarah and his father were still asleep. He gathered himself and went to grab a glass of water. He noticed the chill of the air. The windows were the original sash and his touch against one of the panes of glass felt the coldness outside. Entering the hallway, he made his way past the grandfather clock to the kitchen, having long forgotten, in the haze of muddled consciousness, the event reported by his sister. He wasn't thinking when he looked out of the same window she had gazed through. He experienced nothing. There was just the night, the coldness, the emptiness... but for a shadow that was not his own and not known to him. Michael placed the empty glass on the side and went back to the sitting room. He felt on edge though unsure really as to why.

The shadow that had been with him upstairs watched. A chill ran down Michaels body again. Sarah stirred as he entered but remained asleep. Their father looked comfortable under his warm blanket, murmuring to himself. Michael made a comfier arrangement on the sofa and went back to sleep. The house lay in silence once again. Only the grandfather clock reflected the shadow's presence, witnessing it ascending the staircase.

The morning sun awoke Sarah first. She sensed the light illuminating the room through the windows. She felt rejuvenated after sleeping so well, something she hadn't done in a while. She was so glad Michael was home, she didn't feel alone any more. Michael seemed to sense someone else had risen and he too came to his senses. Their father was still none the wiser.

"So, what's the plan, Stan?" he asked his sister.

"I thought we'd sort breakfast out and see to Dad. Was wondering whether I need to go into the village; might not be wise in this weather, might not even make it."

"Yeah, okay, I'll get the kettle on, get things under way and let you see to Dad. Does he sleep much during the day?"

"He has been but he's getting more active as time goes on."

Michael had already made his way to the door as he listened. He fancied the idea of going into the village. The kitchen came alive with activity, every saucepan, spoon, knife and available hob back in use. Michael had breakfast well and truly under way. The first meal of the day had always held a special sway in his life, an almost addictive quality. If he was happy, he'd treat himself to breakfast; if he was sad, he'd console his mood with breakfast. Anything could warrant a full English. Several times throughout his life he'd had a serious word with himself to try not to lose sight of his belt buckle. But if the buckle could be seen he was in credit and deserved a breakfast, and here he was treating himself after his arduous journey.

Sarah saw the chaos from the door and thought better than to disturb an artist at work, the table already set out and looking good enough to quietly step to one side and take a seat. Among all the activity Michael never thought about the glass he had left there in the early hours, not noticing it was no longer there, moved by means that no physical person had chosen. Sarah put together a light breakfast for their father and returned to start hers with Michael. Tea, coffee, juice, bread, toast, any possible combination associated with breakfast was there. Michael finally realised the glass was missing but assumed it was a casualty of all the culinary chaos and lost to the sea of paraphernalia of a brilliant fry-up. Nothing more was thought of it.

"I fancy a trip into the village. I'll go instead if you like?" said Michael. "But it's a bit dodgy for the car; is dad's old Defender still about?"

"Yeah," replied Sarah, "It's not been used for a little while but it's been wrapped up in the shed; should be fine."

The shed, as it had always affectionately been called, was in fact a little more than that, as one would expect on such a large estate. It was a large outbuilding built when the first motor cars were starting to be seen on the roads and had taken the place of one of the stable blocks. It was mostly empty now but some of the original nuances of the early motoring world were still there as mementoes lucky enough to have survived the onward march of time, in part thanks to their father. The arduous task of clearing up the kitchen was reluctantly started on heavy stomachs.

With everything cleared away, Michael, feeling content, made his way to the shed, the crunch of snow as the layers gave way to his footsteps crisp and loud. The large, solid doors glided open and Michael took in the smells of the building: wood, hessian and oil. He unwrapped the Defender, sweeping away the tarpaulin, propped the bonnet open and reconnected the battery after letting it charge for a while, sipping the warm coffee he'd brought with him from breakfast. It started on the first turn, which came as a pleasant surprise after sitting for so long, but this old girl clearly wasn't going to let him down.

On the way back to the house he caught himself falling into thought. He still didn't know what was going on, and wasn't sure what to make of things. Was someone playing tricks? If so, for what reason? Was someone staking the place out? He decided to track his own footsteps back, gently placing each footstep inside his previous prints from earlier. Not that this would serve much purpose for very long but it made him feel he was in charge, as if he was balancing the scales back in their favour. It made him feel safe; no one could get the upper hand on him!

Upon entering the hall, he could hear his sister talking to their father. He didn't interrupt. Something about his father being in a chair for most of the time and having to relearn what which he had achieved as a baby disturbed him. He didn't want that to happen to him. He went to unpack, choosing one of the front bedrooms on the first floor that had an en suite, and while placing his toiletries in their respective places he thought of his companion. Flint was never far away from his thoughts and he hoped to get back to him soon. Although he knew he was being spoilt rotten and in good hands, it was still sad to be without him.

He called out from the landing, "Sarah! You okay if I pop into the village shortly? I won't be long."

Sarah came out into the hallway, shouting back up, "Yeah, sure. We're just getting the fire stacked up ready for later." She couldn't entirely hide her anxiety. "Be back before dark?" she rhetorically asked but still hoped for a direct answer.

"Oh yeah, definitely," he said, with the best effort at a reassuring tone.

On the road there wasn't much to distinguish between road and verge, between shrub or animal. The snow had covered things well in its invasion of the land and the conquest was almost complete. Michael felt smug in his choice of vehicle. There was enough of a flurry to have the wipers on but the sun still shone through, giving a blinding wintery glare across the windscreen. Reaching the village

Michael took it slowly as he parked in one of the bays that were on a slight slope in front of the row of shops. He popped into one to collect a few essentials and was distracted by the sight of the village pub. I'll have a quick half, he thought. He also rather wondered if anyone would remember him in there. There was no one familiar in the shops; nearly all had been turned into franchises.

"Bless my soul! Well, yours isn't a face I've seen in 'ere for a while." said the landlady in a warm and joyous response to seeing Michael duck through the doorway.

She stood not much taller than the Optics on the bar that she had one hand resting on. She was a good deal older than Michael and probably should have pulled her last pint by now, but it was all she knew and she considered herself to be rather good at it… as did all her customers.

"Hello, Linda!" Michael replied with a cheeky grin. "How's things?" He was surprised how good he felt connecting with someone who recognised him.

"Not bad, can't complain, well at least not about anything anyone's likely to listen to. How are you, my love? Long time no see," she replied, still with great enthusiasm.

"I'm good thanks, Linda, life's going well. I'm back for a little while visiting my sis and checking in on Dad."

"Ah, I did know about your dad, a bastard that! But he's doing well I last heard, reckon he won't be long recovering, be up and 'is old self, you'll see; Linda knows best my sweet."

"I'll have a quick half of Guinness please, Linda."

"Not a problem, my love." She poured with a tilted glass, wiping the base as she pushed it across to Michael.

"There you go my love." she said with another warm smile.

"Linda?" He let out an apologetic laugh. "You've been in this village all your life."

"Oi, what you trying to say," she said with a wink.

He smiled back. "Well, I was wondering: do you know much about our house? Any old tales, that sort of thing?"

"Hmm, not really. Of course, it always lent itself to ghostly tales when it was empty. Before the previous owners who had it, and before your family. Just used to scare each other when we were kids… used to dare each other to break in and look around. Now, I recall, I don't think any of us were brave enough. There was one boy outside our group who got in and climbed the stairs, then lost his nerve before scampering out." Her tone was quieter, more contemplative.

"Why did he lose his nerve? You mean he saw something?" Michael was leaning closer against the bar."

"No", replied Linda, matter-of-factly. "He just got the willies, that's all. Why, you don't believe in that stuff do you?"

Before Michael could reply, she continued. "If you want to know the history to it you need to speak to Jack, or even Sid. He's round the corner nursing a pint as usual."

"Cheers, Linda, I'll go have a word now."

"Sid?" Michael asked tentatively, moving around the bar and unsure if he'd got the right nurser.

"Yes, mate?" the man answered with evident curiosity.

"Mind if I sit down?" Michael asked.

About an hour had passed when, in a momentary lapse in conversation, Michael noticed, through the pub windows, that a flurry of snow was now falling at a steady pace and he wasn't sure if he should stay much longer and run the risk of getting stuck in it. Sid was a historian by hobby and knew some interesting details about the village but only a little about the house. Their house hadn't always been there – that much would have been obvious to anyone – but there had been what Sid called a Wealden hall house, that once stood on the site. Possibly at the beginning of the medieval period. There were rumours of a priory but no one knew for certain. The house itself was old, though, before the Victorian period, further back than the Georgian period. Its current style masked these truths with just subtle hints of its deeper heritage. Where once there were hallways there were now rooms, and rooms that had once been larger spaces. According to Sid there had been many changes over the decades.

Michael mused on all this driving back. Conditions had worsened considerably since his trip into the village and he was hoping he would make it. He'd never let snow stop him before, and with perseverance and stubbornness the house finally came into view through the overworked window wipers, the Land Rover's tyres ploughing fresh furrows into the snow. The sun's light, though dull and obstructed by heavy grey clouds, was aided by the light reflecting from the snow, lending a dense haze to the surroundings. Michael parked the Defender in the shed, snow blowing in from outside and covering the floor. He pulled the doors closed and turned to face the house. Without thinking he looked down to locate the footsteps he had left earlier. But there were none to find. Pointless, he thought, of his clandestine efforts. He made a fresh set of prints as he walked round the side of the house towards where they'd been sitting earlier in the day. A small orange glow shone from the room where his sister and father were. Michael made his way through the side doors from the patio, leaving what was now a blizzard to do its worst.

"Hello! I've just made coffee. I was wondering how you were going to make it back, it came down all of a sudden," Sarah welcomed him.

"Never fear, not got stuck in snow yet," said Michael with a smile as he headed for the kitchen. "You want anything to eat? I fancy something cold; sorry I was so long but I had an interesting chat in the pub."

Sarah gave some coffee to their father and joined Michael in the kitchen. "Really? Surprised anyone recognised you." The friendly jibe at Michael's long absence was not lost on him. He relayed what he had been told before they went back to sit with their father.

The day was drawing to a close quickly, leaving everything apart from for the fire they sat beside obscured by darkness. A still, deep blackness grew, consuming the deepest recesses of the house, enveloping the rooms. The top corridors stretched out into a vacuum, intersected only by each room they passed. Can it be said that if rooms are empty, do they really exist? If there is no one there, no presence to acknowledge they are there, how does one know if they really are there? But within the darkness there was a knowledge that knew. Its presence held the space and intent to make itself known.

CHAPTER THREE

There was a warmth that covered Michael's body as he lay in bed. He loved it when he would naturally wake without an alarm. The necessity to be forced from his slumber because of some worldly commitment always made him feel cheated of some imagined utopia that was snapped away by an early call. It was with deep satisfaction that he now held the contentment within himself as he crunched up his duvet and wrapped his body further into its folds. The room was crisp with the winter morning. It felt nice. It was instinctively natural to him. He knew, unfortunately, he couldn't really stay in this idyll and so began reluctantly summoning up the inclination to remove himself from such comfort and attend to his morning ritual ablutions.

Staring into the bathroom mirror he looked into his reflection. He always saw someone different. He never saw himself in that reflection; his personality didn't feel it matched his corporeal form. Lost in this spell of reflection he heard his sister's footsteps in the corridor outside his room, pulling him from this odd enchantment; but on opening the bedroom door there was no one there to see. She couldn't have covered the distance in that time to now be out of sight, he thought. He closed the door, puzzled; he was certain he had heard footsteps. Dismissing the thought, he returned to the bathroom, to find the hairs on the back of his neck and arms were standing upright. He brushed his arms as if to wipe away an uncomfortable feeling. Michael got dressed. He made no mention of his experience when he was making coffee next to his sister in the kitchen. It didn't seem worth revisiting, and besides he wasn't sure now if he had heard anything at all.

"Sleep okay?" he asked.

"Yes, woke up once or twice through the night, bit tired to be honest but I'm okay," Sarah replied.

Michael was enjoying his first coffee so much that he refilled the stovetop coffee maker and set it to boil ready for another. They both sat down at the table.

"So", Michael started, "before that night, whatever it was – a visitation I suppose – I want to double check: you never felt an unease about the place; Dad hasn't mentioned anything?"

"No, nothing before what I told you about. This place has always felt like home, until recently. Have you sensed something?" she replied.

He didn't confess his experience at the bedroom door. He wasn't sure he wanted to; not yet anyway.

"No nothing." (The faint laughter he'd heard when he first arrived didn't seem real enough to mention.) "I'm just pondering on my conversation with Sid."

They got breakfast going and afterwards went about their separate tasks, Sarah downstairs and Michael out in the workshop. The day had started with some welcome warmth in the air, the sun glistening on the snow particles that feathered the window seals and door covings of the outbuilding. It brought a sense of happiness to Michael. Such mornings would raise his spirits and starve his most intrusive thoughts. He liked to potter in a workshop, and going through some of the old tools and equipment brought back memories of his childhood, when he would play at being a mechanic, with imaginary customers coming to collect their cars. The smell of oil and petrol still permeated the air. Adjacent to the shed was an old woodworking workshop, now home to spiders' webs, that still had the shavings on the floor from its long-ago last project. He imagined the smell of the rich varieties of wood that would have once been used, possibly he surmised to help renovate the house.

The snow flurries continued for most of the day, slowly building on what had been laid down before. The hours passed quickly and Michael's internal clock was telling him he had got cold and was now rather hungry; he turned off the light switch (an old-fashioned toggle that befitted the character of the garage), pulled on the door and locked the heavy, somewhat over-engineered hasp with the click of the heavy-duty padlock.

Sarah had once again got the fire going when Michael walked in from hanging his coat on the hook by the back door. She had already settled their father in for the night, making him comfy in his surroundings. Sarah had started a stew earlier in the day and now Michael prepared it, serving the piping hot meal and sitting down to savour it by the crackling fire. With a bottle of good wine they sat quite content at the prospect of the satisfaction to come, of full stomachs.

They were enjoying the last sips from their glasses when the slam of an upstairs door jolted them out of their contentment. Michael and Sarah looked at each other with apprehension, as if trying to understand what they had just heard could mean. SLAM! SLAM! SLAM! Michael leapt out of his chair and ran out of the room to seek out the noise, followed closely by his sister. SLAM! The last sounded so loud it was as if a door had been ripped from its hinges. They stalked up the staircase to reaching the top corridor; expecting to see an intruder. But all was suddenly silent, not a sound came from anywhere, and it was now hard to tell where the sound really did originate from. Michael's heart was pounding; Sarah looked sick from her body's rush of anxiety. Neither spoke. The corridor became illuminated with a flick of the light switch. The sound must have come from close to where they now stood, Michael thought. Tentatively he opened each door of the corridor to investigate, but there was nothing to be seen. Every door was shut. Every room was empty. No one was there, or anywhere.

"Well, that was bloody strange, I don't mind admitting." Michael's voice betrayed an air of nervous vexation.

"What the hell was that all about?" said Sarah with a quizzical frown.

"Don't know, but that was odd, by any stretch of the imagination," he replied, having no option but to acknowledge this strange happening but not wanting to delve any deeper into his sister's thoughts.

They both made their way back to where their dad was sitting: he was sound asleep.

"Bless him," they said in unison and chuckled at the fact that they had done so. It broke the tension of what had just occurred. They sat back down as if in defiance, as if the sound hadn't really bothered them, it was just the wind. Must have been the wind. Certainly wasn't anyone who had got in, the house was definitely secure, so it must have been the wind… mustn't it?

The night drew on and it was time to turn in. After making sure their father was safely asleep, they kept each other company in the kitchen as Michael prepared a hot bedtime drink. Sarah, with cup in hand, made her way up the staircase, trying to keep dark imaginings at bay, until she suddenly felt a presence beside her. She stopped, grasping the handle of her cup tightly in one hand and gripping the banister with the other. The grandfather clock chimed.

There was nothing that could be seen. Yet the feeling of a presence remained, and she still felt as though she had company. Michael could be heard coming from the kitchen, and all at once the feeling evaporated. She was standing perfectly still when Michael appeared in the hall.

"You okay?" he asked.

"Yeah, I just felt as if someone else was here, it was creepy… Ignore me; must still be on edge from earlier," she replied, keen to dismiss what she thought she had felt.

"Yes, bit odd wasn't it, but the wind can do that… I must admit I never checked to see if the windows were secure, bet one of them was open. Bugger! I'll have to see to that before bed."

"I'll come with you; let me take my drink to my room first," said Sarah.

"No, it's fine, you get to bed, mate, it won't take me long." Michael's reply rang with a confidence that would soon fade when he was on his own, alone in the corridor, checking empty rooms with the hope of finding an open window.

Michael held his nerve with a purposefully nonchalant walk along the corridor. Opening each door; he scouted the rooms more quickly than his imagination could take hold with some dark amusement of its deepest, darkest fantasies. His chances of finding an open window diminishing, he opened the last door, flicking the light switch to show just a small sideboard against the wall and a chair in the corner. The window firmly shut, proven with a forceful shudder of the window latch. Michael began feeling cold as his thoughts started to wander to what exactly could have caused a slamming door without any intervention. Feeling alone now, he urgently wanted to leave the room as a tingling sensation ran the course of his spine, motivating him to action. He stopped off at his sister's room and knocked on the door.

A muffled reply showed that Sarah was deep into her teeth-cleaning ritual. "Yep, I'm okay, all good in here, I'm alright."

Michael went to his room satisfied with one thought: Sarah seemed better for having him with them at the house. He settled into his bed, wrapped himself up in the duvet, turned off the bedside light and closed his eyes.

Sarah too settled in and turned her light off. The rooms, corridors, hallway; the whole house lay in the shadow of the night.

Time passed and Michael had fallen into a deep sleep. So entrenched was he in his slumber that to gather coherent thought would be difficult, but that's what his body was attempting to do now. Something was knocking on his psychological door to wake him up; something's wrong! He began to stir, slowly lifting his senses.

He opened his eyes and moved his head, then slowly pulled himself upright and stared into the darkness. The room that he knew so well was now unfamiliar as he tried to focus his sight, barely able to make out his surroundings. The darkness corrupted his vision,

He was not alone, he felt it.

He stretched out his arm from beneath its warm cover and turned on the bedside lamp. It gave out a bright blast of light. The room was cold. His arms tingled with the lifting of his hairs. He remained quite still, all bar the movement of his eyes as they scanned the room. The sense of a presence in the room remained. He found he couldn't utter a sound. The floorboards creaked as if someone was walking on them. The light flashed even brighter then turned off. The creaking of the floorboards continued. Michael fumbled, searching for the switch again, but he couldn't make the lamp work. In the darkness he felt a heaviness overcome his body. It was as if someone had lain down on top of him. He imagined he was staring into the eyes of this invisible being that was making itself known in this menacing nighttime visit. Fear gripped him in his bed: desperately wanting this to be over, Michael tried the light again. This time it worked and the room lost its threatening atmosphere as the light took away the dread. He found he could move again. He drew up courage and got out of bed.

He opened the bedroom door and tentatively made his way down the corridor, still fearing that what had just happened wasn't over yet.

Getting to Sarah's room he hesitated, and was about to enter when he thought better of it. He decided not to disturb her, thinking it was for the best not to unnerve her more than she already was. He turned to return to his room but realised he needed a drink, so he left his sister's door and continued to the top of the stairs, constantly looking back, his eyes darting from door to door, room to room. He made his way down to the kitchen making sure everywhere was lit. Getting to the kitchen he closed the door firmly.

In his arrogance, Michael assumed only he had been visited. Unknown to him, in that very moment, his sister lay asleep with the figure now visiting her. Without making its presence known to Sarah's subconscious it lay above her, looked at her. Sarah had no clue of this monstrous thing now in her company. It stayed; only vanishing when Sarah started to stir.

It was seven in the morning when Sarah came into the kitchen, opening the door and seeing Michael sitting at the kitchen table.

"Oh, Christ sake! God, you made me jump," she said.

Michael looked at her. "I had a visitor last night; something was in the room with me. I know not what, but something came a-calling."

Sarah stood quietly, looking at Michael.

"This place is haunted!" he stated, staring thoughtfully back at his sister.

It wasn't clear if what her brother had just said had reassured her or unnerved her. It was one thing telling her brother about her fears, someone who didn't really believe in such things and so could find an answer for her, but it was another thing entirely to have him also believe and now confirm that the things being seen were not intruders, not someone to turf out or call the police to deal with. Something else was indeed making itself known.

They decided to make up a bed in the large downstairs room so they could stay together and alert each other should either one have something happen to them. Without realising it they were already hunkering down, as if preparing a bunker against an unknown enemy.

The day passed without incident and they settled in for another night uncertain what, if anything, would come visiting. They were each positioned in their makeshift bed, quietly watching the fire give its warm glow to the room. Their father was fast asleep. It had snowed hard during the day and a fresh deep blanket of virgin snow now swept up at the house, touching the ground-floor window ledges. Michael was gazing into his glass of whisky thinking of Flint and how he could do with his mate beside him now. He knew Flint would most likely be by an open fire right now, content and with a full, furry belly, probably snoring away, muffling the sound of his dog farts. Michael lost himself in reverie thinking about this and let out a little chuckle of amusement when he thought of this habit. Flint's were particularly lethal and could strip a person's nostrils before they knew it.

He got up and busied himself by banking up the fire to keep it burning through the night. Propping himself back in his little indoor camp he noticed Sarah had fallen asleep. He pondered on their situation. What was it that was visiting them? What had gone on in this house to provoke these things now and never before? What had been here before the house? Did that matter? He wanted to sleep but he felt compelled to keep his mind on the door and his surroundings. It was three in the morning when he began to close his eyes, and all was still and quiet.

Without anyone in the room being aware, a ghostly figure, more than just a presence, began to stalk the staircase, itself discordant with its dark surroundings, halting at the top before fading into the wall. The grandfather clock stood as the only witness once again.

Sarah was the first to wake, around seven in the morning. Looking briefly towards their father then over to Michael she went, a little nervously, to make a drink. Both men were awake when she re-entered the room with a large teapot on a tray.

"Morning," she said.

Through the fog of sleep, both acknowledged her morning greeting. "Ah lovely, you read my mind, sis, in need of a decent brew."

Their father shuffled to get comfortable and gratefully accepted a steaming mug and plate of biscuits.

"We won't be going anywhere with this snow," announced Michael.

"I doubt we'll be going anywhere anytime soon," replied Sarah.

Without saying a word, they acknowledged that they would be trapped in the house. A house that now seemed to have taken on a presence all of its own. It had started to feel heavy. Oppressive even. They now both assumed this unknown visitor was somewhere in the house.

After a light breakfast, Michael went out to the woodshed to stock up on logs to bring into the house. On returning to the shed he sat down on a log pile and sipped his tea. From this position he could see most of the rear of the house, and he surveyed each window, deep in thought. His own mood was also heavy. The dark clouds of depression were on the attack. It was starting to take a lot of energy, after so many years, to defend himself against his intrusive thoughts; so far, he was still just about winning. At this time of year, when most people would find the winter months difficult, Michael found comfort; he loved the autumn as well. His thoughts went back to his ghostly experience but he found he had to concentrate harder than before and now he was questioning his own senses… had he really sensed something? Was it just a lucid dream? And the banging of the door, he was no longer clear on that. But perhaps, he thought, it was real and his natural defences were trying to convince otherwise.

He stayed a few more moments before going back inside. Sarah had built up all the fires in the downstairs rooms and turned the central heating on. Their father was practising the exercises prescribed by his physiotherapists, and she had a fresh pot of coffee on. Michael came back in with a determined face. He wanted to know the true history of this house, and had decided to ask his dad what he knew.

It was difficult for their father to speak. He was still finding the basics an enormous effort. He managed to scribble a brief note: 'Paperwork in back office.' Michael went there immediately.

The office had an imposing desk as a central point that drew your attention when you entered the room. There were files stacked neatly on the top shelves. An eclectic mix of novels filled a free-standing bookshelf. There was an old antique chest positioned on the floor up against the wall. In it, Michael found a large clump of paperwork tied together in a ribbon. Kneeling by the chest, Michael unwrapped the bundle and thumbed through the layers with his right hand. It held modern documents as well as deeds dating back over a hundred years. Like a deck of cards, he shuffled them back, picked the ribbon up, went downstairs to the dining room and spread the paperwork out across the large table. Michael loved history and couldn't wait to start looking through it all. But first he had to put a pot of coffee on. It was a ritual of his whenever paperwork was involved. To him it was a form of comfort, much like a smoker might feel setting out their smoking paraphernalia. And no matter how much he was looking forward to it, this task promised him a furrowed brow.

Whenever he had work to do that involved sitting down and concentration then he needed a coffee by his side.

He earnestly scanned the paperwork, sprawling his fingers across the separate sheets. The intricate writing of the older documents excited Michael. The oldest showed that the house they knew today was largely built in the Georgian period by a Mr Tolhurst. He had made most of his fortune through the sugar plantations and slavery, a source of income that was excepted among the business elites of the day but details were little known to others. The house back then employed forty-two servants including the butler and under butler. Forty-two! Michael ran that number through his head and began to imagine what it must have been like in those days, the lives that had been lived in the very place he now sat. He wished he could travel back in time just to witness the hustle and bustle of it all.

Reading on, he found the name Eleanor, the wife of Mr Tolhurst, and four children making it into adulthood. Four more, according to the attached death certificate, did not, dying early in their young lives. Michael pondered on this particular detail. There were further occupants and a long list of names of people associated with the house. Then Michael found a plan of the original footprint of the house what was the new Georgian extension had been built on. Some of the lines overlaid perfectly onto the old plan, some of the lines carried on beyond the boundaries, but it also showed two long lines extending away from where the new footprint existed, off in the direction where Sarah had seen something that night.

Michael's heart raced, coming up with a theorised answer before his brain could switch into gear. He got up to fetch his sister. As he left the table, he noticed a small scrap of paper that had slid across the polished surface from the original bundle. Picking it up, he read the beautiful hand-written script.

House built on medieval site. Oubliette still intact.

Michael stopped… his heart gave out palpitations. His internal monologue read out the message again.

He'd never suspected the existence of a dungeon. Was that what an oubliette was? But where could it be? And who had written this note? What was the significance of it? Holding the paper in one hand he felt compelled to carry on searching through the rest of the documents, glancing at each one but finding nothing that spoke so loudly as the note.

"Sarah!"

"What is it?" She hurried in through the doorway.

"Look at this, I found it amongst this lot." He held out the note to her.

"An oubliette!?" she said in a quizzical fashion. "Isn't that a torture hole?"

Michael frowned at the note. "Is it? Well, clearly we have to find it, Sarah, if it exists that is; but why would there be a note if the dungeon doesn't exist?"

"So it is a dungeon?"

Michael grew a little irritated at his excitement becoming bogged down in detail. "Dungeon, hole, pit; whatever it is it must be found."

"I don't know, Michael. How do we even start to look for it, are we going to start ripping up the floorboards?"

The thought had never occurred to Michael that it might be in the house.

"No, I don't know, but it's on the to do list!" he said with keen enthusiasm.

Gulping down the remains of his now cold coffee he went outside to survey the white- covered land, leaving Sarah without a backward glance or a thank you. It can't be in the house, he thought. Finding such a thing might be impossible in the best of conditions, but right now it seemed a mere fantasy in all this snow. But Michael had a new determination about him, a renewed energy that was keeping the darker thoughts at bay. He was both excited and puzzled. Would he be able to find this oubliette?

That night they sat down to eat a concoction of food picked from the fridge along with some pasta. A glass of white and the fire again for company. Their father was enjoying what he could of the meal and

Sarah held his glass while he took little sips. As they sat in their makeshift camp there was nothing but silence. The room was absorbed in a warm glow. The rest of the house lay once again in deep darkness.

Outside, the outbuildings took on an abandonment of their own. A fox was sauntering by the shed doors. The estate reflected in a brilliant haze from the night snow. You could see far off into the distance from the light. The shed, all alone, held an empathy for the house and kept its contents safe. The upper echelons of the great house lay empty and cold. Each room was void of any presence. The clock observed no movement. The night seemed to pass without any protest to the day.

All were in a deep sleep when the sun rose once again. Sarah stirred slowly, resisting the need to get up. But when she stood at the doorway of the kitchen, wrapped in her dressing gown, she became rooted to the floor, frozen with anxiety and fear. Before her eyes was a figure, highlighted by the bright haze coming through the window. It seemed to be going about its own business but its movements didn't line up with the furnishings, as though it was living in a different time when the room had a different function. The figure was hunched, a darkened shadow that didn't appear to have any discernible face. It didn't seem to be aware of Sarah's presence. It then looked to the side as if in acknowledgement and quickly vanished.

Sarah calmed down as she gathered her thoughts on what she just witnessed. The fear left her as quickly as it had come. She realised there was no malice in her feelings, she felt no sense of evil, only… pity. That was it, pity. She felt an overwhelming sense of sadness, of loneliness, isolation and hurt. Who or what was this figure? Where had it come from? What era even? Sarah, though, felt a sense of calm. A strange juxtaposition to the event.

"Michael," she whispered, returning to the room. "Is Dad awake."

"No, not yet, sound asleep, what's up?" Michael replied.

Sarah sat down beside him. "I've just seen something in the kitchen… a ghost. In the daylight, Michael, a real ghost. Only this time it wasn't some horrid visitation, just a figure that seemed to be occupied. Yes, occupied that's it. It was weird, yet right now I feel calm not scared. Michael, it's the weirdest sensation."

Michael listened intently. He saw her eyes glisten.

"Well, that's decided," he declared. "It's haunted, this place is bloody haunted, and I mean it this time. Question is, how many of them are there?" He said this with a pensive grin.

Sarah returned to the kitchen to make tea, somehow confident she wouldn't encounter the figure again, at least not now. Michael joined her and began preparing breakfast. Afterwards he called Mary to see if she was alright and Flint was being a good boy. It went straight to voicemail.

"Hello, it's Mary, well, not really dear, ooh now what am I doing 'ere... Hello!?"

Michael chuckled to himself; bless her. He would call later and hopefully all would be well. He stepped outside to feel the cold air and appreciate the snow, that had taken on a fluffy candy-floss appearance. It had crystallised, having encountered only cold wind and no more fall. He sipped his coffee in a somewhat contented mood, his thoughts turning over the imagined history of the land he was now standing on. Time to sort this out, he thought, tapping the side of his cup with his forefinger.

CHAPTER FOUR

The next morning started early. Michael had busied himself clearing a path through the snow from the house down to the entrance of the drive. Individual mounds of snow now lined the edges, the differing size clumps indicating bursts of enthusiasm interspersed by resting breaks. Vehicles could now get through with relative ease. Steam rose from the top of his head when he removed his woollen hat. Inside, Sarah was reading some of the documents in detail while their father was doing some of his exercises from the physio. All would have seemed normal if it was not for their recent experiences.

Michael went to the shed, where glancing downwards he noticed the unmistakable paw prints of the visiting fox. With a smile he cleared a little patch on the ground and left two eggs in a sheltered bowl for whenever the fox might appear again. It satisfied Michael knowing he was offering some relief from the harsh reality of life for a creature that had enough to deal with just surviving. He didn't often worry about weather conditions but with it being so bad this year he found the old snow chains his dad had stored and busied himself putting them on the Defender. A task that was difficult until he got to the last wheel and finally remembered how it was meant to be done. Once the job was completed he tried Mary again.

"'Ello?".

"Hello, Mary? It's Michael."

"Oh hello, dear, how are you?"

"I'm well thank you, still here with my sister and dad, just wanted to check in with you and see how Flint was?"

"Yep, my dear, still fine this end. I think he's settled right in, he won't want to go home," she said with a trailing chuckle.

"I am grateful, I really appreciate it, I hate to put on you but I think I'm gonna be stuck here for a while."

"Oh, that's fine dear, you do what you have to. We'll still be okay 'ere, 'hope you're okay though."

"Yeah, I'm okay, thank you so much, Mary, much appreciated."

Michael felt a pang of sentiment hit him as he reminisced over Flint. He missed his companion very much. But after a moment of contemplation about his BFF, the picture of the layout in the documents came back into to his mind. He wanted to see if there was anything discernible on the ground, or that could give some information in connection with the note. Surely if there was anything, they would have found it as kids. He started to walk away from the house in the direction he thought was the right one. In attempting to kick through the icy layer of snow that had cemented itself like an eggshell to the grass and rotten leaves he noticed a faint line in the wooded area. Nothing obvious at first, just a subtle change in growth, and perhaps a thing only noticeable in adulthood. Ducking under a low-hanging branch into the woodland he traced the line, still surprised not to have any recollection of it as a child. He must have ventured this way; what young boy wouldn't investigate a wood? Must have been a lost memory, he supposed. Using a large stick, Michael prodded at the ground and swept away the icy leaves looking for anything that might look out of place in the natural surroundings. All at once he found himself flying into the brambles and disappeared head first into a mass of rotten leaves. A large stone had been the culprit, mostly buried but protruding just enough to send Michael on his unexpected trip. Somewhat annoyed with himself and instantly with the world, as one is when an inanimate object gets the better of them, he composed himself and started clearing away the detritus of the woodland floor. He traced the outline of the exposed part. The stone appeared to have no obvious limit, and the more he cleared and dug away, the more of it became visible. Another stone was revealed jointed neatly against this one, then another. They seemed to be coping stones of significant size. Michael stood up and could see that a clear path was forming. The ground was solid for the most part but there was a section that felt softer, the earth was deeper. Was this it? Some random broken path before him? Was this some ancient pathway to the hell of an oubliette? Without allowing himself to think he quickly went back to get a spade.

On his return he struck the ground with zeal, flinging the frozen earth any which way his arms chose to deposit the load.

CLANK!

The spade had struck stone. Using his hands as trowels Michael pushed away the earth. Another stone! Before long Michael was standing at the top of three cleared steps leading down from where he stood. His emotions were racing like a child. Digging even faster, his actions became frantic as each new step was discovered. Deeper now; Michael had to look up from what he counted was the eighth step. He had a sense of being in an open grave, and looked around him. He was now in a small stairwell with ancient stone walling that descended with each step. One thought shouted to him… Sarah had to see this! It was the oubliette!

Kneeling on one of the steps he took a brief moment and considered what he may have actually uncovered. The torments that could have occurred, the last moments that someone might have felt, descending from the external world into this underworld. He snapped himself out of his reverie. It was after all just a set of stone steps. It was just as likely to be an old ice house. He knew that if it hadn't been for the note then an ice house would be exactly what he would be expecting. But he allowed his id personality to take the lead.

"Sarah!?" Michael shouted as he ran through the hallway.

"SARAH!" He yelled with even more urgency, and some annoyance at having not yet been answered.

"In here! Michael, look at this—" She was cut short.

"You've got to come and see what I've just found, come on, come on!"

"Wait!" she barked back, her own temper stoked by her brother's dismissal. "Look at this." She was pointing to a piece of paper.

Michael stood like a petulant child, his id firmly put in its place.

A frown appeared on Sarah's face. "Look… it says here that the house was built over the top of a Wealden hall. Didn't you say that Sid guy said there was a Wealden hall here? And more, look. It mentions there was a burial place, Saxon maybe, who knows even older perhaps, somewhere in the grounds."

Sarah was evidently in her own state of euphoria over what *she* had discovered.

Michael's face looked back in equal astonishment. "Oh my God, Sarah, you have so got to see what I've found." Sarah's new evidence had dismissed an idea of an ice house; it must be the oubliette, or a burial place. He grabbed the paper from Sarah's hand and moved swiftly to the back door.

"Wait a minute, Michael, for Christ's sake let me get my coat and boots on!"

Sarah's preparations for the cold gave Michael time to grab a second spade. "You'll need this!" he said, handing it to her as she came out of the house.

Sarah's expression suggested that her main use for a spade might be to clobber Michael round the head with it, but instead she followed her brother into the woods.

"Look at this!" he proudly exclaimed, standing at the top of the discovered steps.

Sarah yanked up the shovel. "Well, this is starting to make more sense," she said.

There was a fluttering of snow in the air as they proceeded to scrape away and make clean each new step that was revealed. They were several steps down when earth began to fall and backfill the stairwell, but by now they had revealed the top of an arch, the keystone clearly visible. They intensified their efforts, eventually revealing a door. What was in front of them now was evidently something very old. It was made of wood, by the look of it very thick, showing signs of decay. There was no discernible opening, no lock or hinges. They scanned it with their eyes and felt the surface with their hands. Sarah used the edge of her spade to scrape an outline of the door. In doing so the spade got caught. She had found a latch hidden under the dirt and set within the wall.

They looked at one another before she prised at it with the edge of the spade. The effort sprung the door from its shut position; it was only a release from its frame but there was enough of a gap to continue to work the stone edging loose and squeeze a set of fingers through the fissure. Pulling it open revealed a dark void, a tunnel that dropped away to a steep decline. No steps, just a rough cobbled surface. Using the light on his phone Michael shone what little light it gave into the depths of the darkness; no end to the passage could be judged.

After all this work the day was drawing to a sharp close. Excitement mixed with frustration they pushed the door closed. The remaining snow that had hung in the air all day was starting to fall more heavily and already starting to rebury the steps.

"Bugger this weather, I want to know what's down there!" Michael said with wide, excited eyes.

"It must be what the note refers to… the oubliette," Sarah replied with equal excitement.

The snow made an eerie crunching sound as they stepped up out of the stairwell, like a lucky escape for a lost soul of antiquity from the world of Hades. Sarah wondered if Cerberus would be at the bottom of the slope waiting patiently for their return.

"God, hope Dad's been alright," she said as they walked back into the house and into a blast of warm relief.

Their father was where they had left him. He gave them a gentle thumbs up to show he was okay. Michael set about restocking the fire and Sarah went to warm the oven ready for a makeshift supper from the freezer.

That evening their minds raced, examining every possible answer while they ate dinner. Their father was warm and comfortable, nodding off to sleep as the fire licked the throat of the flue. The warm glow of the kitchen light shone earnestly out into the external darkness. Michael happened to look up and out of the window while clearing the table.

Softly he said to Sarah, who had followed him into the kitchen, "Look, there's someone moving out there."

Sarah, not without apprehension, turned to look. She had no doubt that it was the same figure that had terrified her and prompted her phone call that night. She covered her mouth to stifle her alarm and whispered, "That's the thing I saw." She moved back from the window, refusing to look at it again.

Michael, not having had his sister's experience, continued to watch. His inner voice was telling him to look away but he couldn't help but fix his gaze. To Michael the figure did appear to be ghostly, showing only as a dark silhouette against the background of the wooded tree line. All of a sudden it disappeared. Then, quicker than a blink of an eye, it was back. Standing still, darker than its surroundings, not moving at all. Between the woods and the house, it just remained, in the middle of the open landscape of the gardens.

Michael felt the dread first. There was a true sense of desolation. The fear entered his very being, just like it had done with his sister. And then it was gone, along with the figure. Almost instantly Michael began questioning his senses, such was the instantaneous dissipation of what had just happened.

"So that was the thing you saw." A statement rather than a question, but Sarah answered nonetheless.

"Yes, and I had hoped to never see it again."

"And it was the thing I sensed in my bedroom; I got the same feeling of dread." He shuddered. "God, that means it's not just outside... it's in here with us, Sarah."

That night they stayed downstairs again, still fearing being alone in their individual bedrooms. They were far from recapturing their home from whatever was obviously there with them. But they had found the stairway, and with a fresh new zeal the next day they would prepare to enter the tunnel!

CHAPTER FIVE

They had prepared themselves to the fullest extent that an amateur cave explorer could do with limited resources. Sarah had heard once something about gases that could render you unconscious in places that had been unopened for a long time, so it was decided one of them should go down first. Michael volunteered. Sarah reminded him of their weight disparity and asked how the hell, exactly, she would be able to pull him back up? She would go first. They anchored ropes to the floor at the top of the steps by covering them with the heaviest rocks they could find, on the basis that the weight and ultimately a fair dashing of hope would pin them down. Sarah looped her end of the rope around her waist, then over her shoulders. She hung a large work light at her side and turned it on.

"Right, you okay?" Michael asked her, grabbing the rope tight and looping it around his body.

"Yes, fine… time to go." Sarah's confident tone sounded as if she knew exactly what she was doing. But her heart was pounding. With her brother's help she lowered herself down the slope of the descending passageway, gripping with both feet and holding on to the sides. She felt a giddy sickness but reminded herself that they needed to know what it was that they had found.

Part of their detailed planning was to establish light as they went. Michael became aware of how comical it looked as Sarah began pinning Christmas tree lights nervously to the wall with one hand. They had taken all they could find and trailed them from an extension lead plugged into an old generator in the shed.

Michael became less of a companion as she progressed, remaining at the top of the opening. She was feeling more and more isolated. Looking into the darkness there was no clue to when it would end. The shaft continued. Try as she might to suppress her fears and stop overthinking, she couldn't help but wonder what might be waiting for her in the blackness. Was this where the terrifying figure came from? A once poor soul tormented at the bottom of this slope in nothing more than a crippling cell? No! she thought, put it out of your head my girl, just get on with the job! She was irritated with herself for letting fear into her thoughts. The soft stone underfoot crumbled and broke away slightly with each movement of her feet, the smell reminiscent of an old castle, which induced her to recall school trips when they would run through the ancient corridors and turrets of once mighty and impregnable fortresses. She liked this smell; it calmed her nerves; for a moment all she could think of was the gift shop where you could buy a castle-shaped pencil rubber.

It had felt like an eternity had passed by the time she reached a wall at the base of the passage. Michael was a distant silhouetted form at the top, still with rope in hand.

"I've hit bottom!" she shouted back up. Looking round, "At least I think I have."

"What can you see?!" Michael shouted back in frustrated excitement.

"Hang on! No, Michael, there's stairs! There are stairs!" she shouted.

"Don't go any further!" he said.

"Not much fear of that," she muttered to herself. "I'm shattered." Adrenaline now giving way to anxiety; stuck at the end of a shaft in near darkness with more stairs disappearing to who knows where. Or who knows what!

"We'll get you back up and rig something up so we can both use the tunnel."

Sarah was heaved unceremoniously out of the opening.

"Well done, that was amazing!" Michael congratulated her.

Sarah was relieved at getting out but damn well proud of herself too. They both peered back into the tunnel. The Christmas lights were doing a surprisingly good job.

"So," Sarah started, "there is a base, like a landing." She pointed with her finger. "But the stairs lead down even further to the right, just out of view. I could only count about five or six but there are probably more."

"My God! We've found something special here, sis, we're proper little archaeologists."

They closed the door tightly, this time making sure to wedge one of the large rocks that had previously helped hold Sarah up, against it, and made their way back to the house. From a distance they were watched leaving by a presence, one that now was becoming bolder.

They quickly checked their father was okay and set about constructing a ladder in the workshop, with the idea that it would lie flat on the tunnel floor and butt up against the wall Sarah had found. As it took shape it reminded Michael of a First World War tunnelling system that the solders had used to attack each other's enemy lines.

The day was getting on once more but they were desperate to get back to the tunnel. They trudged through the snow carrying each end of their new climbing frame, reopened the door and slowly lowered the ladder down the slope.

"Perfect!" they declared in unison and gave a chuckle at their perfect timing.

"Let's get down there before the day beats us again!" said Michael.

They stood at the base of the tunnel on a rough stone step where they could stand upright shining their torches down the newly found second stairwell. The ceiling was rounded and low. Perhaps there had once been a door or gate but now there was just an opening to the next set of steps. There was an earthy smell. Roots penetrated the walls and snaked across the steps. Their hearts were pounding with excitement and trepidation as they descended. At the bottom there was another archway, very thick in depth with evidence of another door, also now missing. Walking through, having to stoop as they went, Michael's torchlight cut through the darkness and exposed a wall on the far side. Sarah helped with her torch and they began to get a better sense of their surroundings.

There were more roots, thicker and larger, criss-crossing the walls like veins of a monster that had swallowed them both. Shining the lights upwards there were roots twisting their way downwards like stalactites from the vaulted ceiling. Neither spoke as they continued to edge through the pitch black, seeing only glimpses of what the torchlight revealed. They eventually traced the border of the room, partly by torchlight and partly by scuffing their feet against the walls and floor. It was a large room. The end wall had fetters lying against it, rusted and decayed after years of abandonment. Their expedition suddenly felt very ominous. They had found the oubliette, surely, but this was larger than such a chamber ought to be.

Before either had uttered a word, their hearts simultaneously jumped. In the corner was a small opening, perhaps half Michael's height. Moving the torch they could see the opening led inwards. On his knees Michael strained his eyes to see.

"You cold? I'm bloody freezing," said Sarah, moving from one foot to the other.

Michael concurred. But although it was cold, uncomfortably so, he was transfixed by this opening. Sarah shone the light about the room as Michael scraped at the earthy blockage to this opening.

"We need to find what this is. We need some more gear."

It was undoubtedly creepy in this dark underground world and they were both sensing it. Before they let their imaginations take hold they decided to leave and get better prepared.

Like old miners they emerged from their expedition, disconnected the lights and the tunnel disappeared into the darkness once again. The door was pushed closed and secured by placing the stone back. Michael didn't want any wildlife falling in, though he was not so fused about humans; they could look after themselves.

Tugging on the door to check its security Michael turned to Sarah. "I can't believe Dad doesn't know anything about this."

Sarah leapt to their father's defence. "He may not do. I mean, it's out here away from the house, and even with all the renovations that have gone on it could have been overlooked. Unless you think Dad discovered it and then reburied it?"

"He could have done, maybe didn't want us finding it, but I suppose you're probably right," her brother replied. "But strike me, what have we just found? Its bloody amazing. And I'd like to know who wrote that note, and when they wrote it. They knew it was here, whoever they were."

He stopped and looked directly at Sarah. "And if they knew, why did they cover it up? There's something odd here."

"Yes, nothing about this feels right," agreed Sarah.

They made their way back to the house. Inside, their father was sleeping. Sitting at the dining table discussing what had been found so far, they made a list.

Floodlight, maybe two or three

Another shovel

Loppers, for the roots

Buckets

Rope

Proper lights for the tunnel

Waterproof trousers

(Get some food)

"Reckon that'll do the job," said Sarah.

"Yep. I'll pop into the village for it, but probably best to leave it till tomorrow, see how this weather settles in I guess?" Michael replied.

They decided to use what little remained of the day to head back to the entrance and see if there was anything observable above ground. They traced where they thought the underground room they had found would be under their feet, pushed the snow away with their feet and snapped off overhanging branches. It was surreal to now know there was a void beneath them. It was proving hard to see and they were feeling frozen now. There was nothing clear to be seen. Whatever had been there before was certainly now gone. There must have been a building, they thought, something at least to connect to what they had found. They gave up on the day and returned to the house.

CHAPTER SIX

Michael barely ate his breakfast. It was early and it was unlike him not to eat but his thoughts had overtaken his hunger.

"I'll be back soon." He pulled on his wax coat. "As soon as I've got what we need. Hopefully the snow will stay away."

"Just take your time, no point ending up in a ditch; the thing will still be here," replied Sarah.

She hoped he would be back soon. She didn't like to show it as much as Michael did but she had to admit, she wanted to resolve the mysteries regarding their new find. She also didn't want their father and her to be left on their own for too long. Standing at the entrance of the great house she watched until the back of the Land Rover disappeared from view.

Something else was watching too. The ominous presence was looking out from one of the upper windows.

The tyre chains did their job as Michael set out, but it took a little longer to get to the village owing to the conditions. He cautiously navigated the snow-laden car park at the centre of the village. The conspiracy theory held that the building that once stood there was burnt down, allowing the council to gain revenue from the parking lot, although no one ever bothered to check the validity of the story.

It had snowed hard and everywhere was white. There wasn't much footfall and any cars that had ventured out had been left in the grips of the snow. Michael amused himself on observing that the village snowman had now gained some new appendages.

Thankfully the hardware store was open, next to the post office with brass overhead lamps across the signage. The bell rang when Michael opened the door. A smart, elderly gentleman dressed in a shirt and tie with a brown front-buttoned dust coat stood behind an open counter that had a brass measuring rule inlaid at the edge.

"Michael!?" said the gentleman, looking for assurances that his eyes were not misleading him.

"Hello, John… blimey, I didn't expect you to still be working here."

"Only just; I retire in another six months. I didn't know you were back. How are you?" asked John.

"Not bad, just back visiting for a little bit and popped in to pick some bits up… doing a bit of work for Dad and helping my sister out."

"Ah yeah, that's nice, bloody shame your dad being the way he is… goes to show you never know what cards are marked for you."

After a longer chat than he'd intended and John's help with picking the items he needed from the stock on the shelves, Michael was helped to his car. Once the food shopping was done, he was on his way home. The roads were turning icier, and even with the snow chains it was a steady cautious journey.

Sarah, who was sitting with their father, heard the return of the Defender crunching its way up the driveway and round to the back of the house. "Successful trip?" she asked, standing in the doorway in an attempt to keep sheltered from the cold.

"Yep!" he answered, opening the back and pulling out the shopping. "Managed to get everything we need."

"That's good. It's been uneventful here while you've been out." she said, pulling the bags up and taking them inside. She didn't tell Michael about the faint footsteps she thought she'd heard, dismissing them as her paranoid imagination.

Michael carried on sorting things out, double checking he had everything and placing it all inside a garden cart, then put the Land Rover to bed. Stamping his feet on the inside doormat he asked Sarah if she wanted to go down and set things up. Still eager to learn more about what was going on and what they had found, she put on her coat at once.

A small snowdrift had formed at the base of the doorway, covering the stone and forming what looked like a slumped body, which didn't really help their nerves. With the rock out of the way the snow was easily pushed aside as the door opened. Michael went first with a work torch to aid the incongruously pretty Christmas lights. Sarah passed down the floodlights before making the descent herself. All was going well so far. Before they ventured down the steps and into the room, they set up appropriate lighting in the first tunnel. Now everything was brightly illuminated and with spades in hand they scraped away the roots on the steps as they went. The room accepted the warm glow from the beam of light on the small landing, which made it seem a lot less threatening than before. As they turned on the other lights to illuminate their surroundings, Michael saw that the room had not diminished from the impressions of their previous visit, but this time the full wonder was on display.

The vaulted ceiling looked beautiful, the bosses on the sides possibly indicating it may once have had a grander importance in its long life. The fetters were clearly visible now but even more gruesome, now it was illuminated, was a torture cage hanging from a rather precarious gibbet.

"Oh my God!" Sarah took a step back.

"At least it's empty," Michael commented ruefully.

Set within the centre wall they now saw a beautiful caryatid that looked as though it had once supported something larger. It was intricately carved, but roots and tendrils now almost covered the evidence of the figure's long labour. It was as if she had been purposefully encased within the wall. There was something sad about this stone figure; Sarah empathetically pulled away the tendril covering her face.

Leaving her to her solemn reverence, Michael shone his light across the wall to find the opening in the corner. Deeper inspection proved it was blocked by roots and earth along with some fallen masonry. He stabbed at the blockage with his spade, expelling the waste out to the side of his legs, enabling him to burrow further. The spade found a softer patch and Michael pulled the looser earth away. He could see through and found it was only the entrance that had been filled in. Shining the light, he could see that the tunnel continued without hindrance. He was now on his hands and knees scuffling forward with Sarah now crouching down behind, looking on. It smelt like a damp cellar. The floor was hard.

Sarah didn't much like the thought of being left behind so she cautiously followed. Their bodies blocked out most of the benefit of the floodlights left behind, making them reliant on their torches once more. At irregular intervals there were small grates just on the turn of the curved ceiling. Only open now to clumped earth and extruding roots. Michael unconsciously acknowledged them as he passed. It must have taken them twenty minutes to complete the route, coming to the end with another set of ascending steps, though smaller this time and fewer in number. The tunnel was still too restricted for either to stand as they crawled up to another door. This door was just as old as the first and equally solid, but this time slightly ajar. Michael heaved at it, but it moved with remarkable ease. On the other side there was a short corridor, just a little larger than a box room. In the side wall was another door, seemingly primitive in its construction. Sarah was right behind him. The door opened to reveal a lath and plaster wall.

Michael knew they must be back at the house. His suspicions had been building but this was proof. Wondering where they would come out, Michael kicked a hole through the wall, snapping the narrow strips of wood and creating a cloud of dust as his foot breached the divide.

Pushing through the gap, he came out into one of the servants' corridors, opened the rather more sophisticated door opposite and stepped out from under the staircase and into the main hall. Covered in dust, neither of them could quite believe they were now back at the house. How was it that a tunnel had been here all along and they knew nothing about it.

"DAD!" they shouted out to each other. "How would he not know about this?" Michael asked.

Sarah walked off, leaving Michael to guess her intentions. She was clearly running on her emotions. She hastily scribbled on a piece of paper.

Did you know?!

Did you know about a tunnel? A dungeon!?

She showed it to their father, who had clearly been awoken on hearing the crash as Michael kicked his way through the wall.

"There's a tunnel that leads from the house into some underground room; whatever it is we don't know. Do you know, Dad?" she asked with an anxious tone.

Her father looked up from the note with a pensive frown, and murmured the word "crypt". Then added a nod in response to her question.

Sarah got the sense that he was aware of the dungeon, crypt, torture chamber, bloody wine cellar for all she knew, but the tunnel connecting it to the house, it seemed, was a mystery.

She went back out into the hall and bumped straight into Michael who was patting down his clothes and brushing some of the debris away.

"Dad, knew, well knows… about the crypt anyway," she told Michael.

"Bloody hell, so why didn't we know? I mean they were always both so excited about each thing they found here, so Mum must have known too, surely? They were both so enthused with this house I thought they shared everything with us. Obviously not, eh?"

"Obviously not," Sarah agreed, evidently a little put out. The feeling of not being trusted can be upsetting.

"I'm starting to feel there is a past mischief in this house that has been long forgotten, something we're only touching on." Michael looked earnestly at his sister.

Though they wanted to know so much more, the time was passing quickly and neither wanted the opening in the wall they made to stay that way. Michael boarded it up with some marine ply from one of the outbuildings and made everything secure for the night. Another day had moved quickly.

The evening came with an uncomfortable feeling. The house felt very different now. It seemed to them they were intruding in its own land, as though they were trespassers. Their father was fast asleep again, and although they wanted answers they wondered if any more would be forthcoming.

Michael built up the fire until it was roaring away with its reassuring, friendly glow. It was ten o'clock. The room still felt cold, as if it had now grown in size to encompass the tunnel that led all the way to the woods and drew in the cold.

The hands of the hallway clock marched on. Now, with all asleep, the hands passed twelve. The clock stood as always, bearing witness to the night and to the reflection that now stood in front of it. The cloaked figure had returned. But there was something more sinister about it now. It was twisted in some way, somehow more grotesque in its lost features. Its movement was now jarring and painful. It made its way up the stairs, the habit it wore long and draping over the steps. Its presence went before it, summoning the house to wake and be fearful. It was dark, heavy, oppressive.

Michael stirred, panting, heavier in his sleep. He was lost to dreams that were slowly degrading into nightmarish visions. But he could feel and hear his heart beat faster. Sarah too was deep in sleep, lost in her dreams, oblivious to the happenings of the night.

Screams entered Michael's head, dark and ominous; hurt and lowliness filled his very soul. He wanted to wake but his body trapped his consciousness, allowing only dread to enter... there was an echo here of a time past. It was ancient to him. He felt he was about to die.

The figure entered the top corridor and stood in the centre of a bedroom, paused and crouched down. The bedroom door slammed, incarcerating the figure. The sound brought Michael out of his frightening visions. But he was the only one to awaken. He felt frightened and anxious. It was hard to pull himself fully out of sleep and come back to reality. He didn't disturb his sister or father but felt compelled to leave the room. Wondering if he had heard a noise at all.

The hallway was cold and dark. Flipping the switch, the illumination seemed to take away the trepidation he felt. It immediately returned, however, when he looked at the staircase... There were clear footprints: two prints on the first step and then the singular alternating prints that showed someone – or something – was climbing the staircase. He crouched down, squinted his eyes to ascertain whether he was seeing things right. His senses were still in that half-awake, half-asleep state that you sometimes get when trying not to disturb your sleep too much when the call of nature pulls you from your bed. But these were human footprints and he was definitely seeing right. But to make a print there must be a reason. Tapping one of them with his forefinger he tried to tell if it was wet or solid. It was neither. It appeared to be more akin to a thick resin; congealed.

He followed the trail until he was standing where the footprints stopped; at a locked bedroom door. He stood waiting. What for he didn't quite know. He could see his breath; it had become cold… so, so cold! His skin tingled and he felt isolated, at the end of a dark corridor with something that had obviously left a set of prints that now appeared to go into a locked room. How the hell did he keep finding himself in these situations? Slowly he put one foot forward. Arms tight, fist clenched. Then one more step.

"Michael!!" A voice he did not recognise called out to him. His neck withdrew into his shoulders as they clenched and tightened. He wanted to run, just run. He was so full of fear. Who or what had said his name? For a while he remained still, half in step ready to run and half in tension ready to fight.

"Michaeeel." The voice called again, this time almost mocking in tone.

He wanted to be away from that spot. He wished he wasn't there. His inner, most childlike fears had been exposed and now took hold of his mind. All his neural transmitters were sending signals; he was in danger. Every primordial fibre of his body was telling him not to be there. Just like it does when you're a child and afraid of the dark.

Then, the door handle began to move, ever so slowly, creaking as if being tightly gripped. With the release of the latch on the final turn the door slowly opened. He couldn't turn round, couldn't go back. Fighting his fear and indecision he made a snap judgement and stepped forward.

The atmosphere was crippling and it was so cold. His heart was pounding, making his head hurt. He had seen something move as the door opened so he knew whatever it was it was in there.

Now at the opening. He reached out and tentatively pushed the door wide open. He hesitated but his body seem to want the experience done with and he lunged into the room. His mouth open, he gasped at the cold air. His eyes glazed. The figure stood at the window looking out. Michael could tell it knew he was there. Awkwardly, it turned to face him. He felt vulnerable and exposed. The presence rushed at Michael before evaporating into thin air with a blood-curdling scream. Michael fell to the floor as if he had been physically pushed. He propped himself against the wall holding his knees tight, fearful of being trapped in the room should the door slam shut, yet he couldn't move.

To add to these nightmarish happenings, at the far end of the corridor appeared the figure of a child. Perhaps six years of age. Michael was overwhelmed by what he had seen and indeed was still seeing. The child ran down the corridor and vanished at the top of the stairs, which spurred Michael to leave the room and run after it;

only to find nothing but emptiness and a distant echo of haunting giggles.

What was left of his tattered courage finally left him, adrift in the corridor. He seized his only chance of coherent thought and fled down the stairs. Faster and faster until his movement was more of a fall than a controlled run. At the base, hitting the cold floor of the hallway with a final jump from the penultimate step he caught within his periphery something darting through the doorway of the dining room. His nerves were by now shot to pieces but his wanton curiosity drove him to understand, to investigate and to enter the room. He wondered if it was the child.

The room was void of light and upon flicking the switch no relief came: the lights appeared to have blown. Something was in there; he'd seen it go in. As he stood in the doorway looking into the darkness a small figure appeared at the far end of the room. Fear gripped Michael once again. The figure giggled and ran towards the wall, disappearing through it.

That was it! Michael was finished. His senses alive to his fear he now ran across the hallway and into the room where his sister and father were. They were still asleep! In his panic he slammed the door, waking them both.

Sarah was startled. "Michael?"

Michael stood with his back to the door looking painfully ill, all colour drained from his face, his eyes alert and scared. None of them moved or spoke, waiting for another to break the silence.

"I don't know what the hell I've just seen, or think I've seen," said Michael at last.

Sarah looked at her brother.

"Yur, yur, yoouu've seen… it too, then?" their father haltingly asked.

Michael fixed his eyes on his father and Sarah turned her head to see.

"Seen what exactly, Dad?" There was accusation in his voice.

"I o-o-only know of a child… it's not made itself known… for a long time. Sss-Sod this bl-bloody body." The old man dammed himself for not having the strength to say more.

"It's okay, Dad," said Sarah, instinctively knowing her father's male pride was hurting as much as his body was.

Sarah looked at her brother. "What's happened, Michael? Where have you been?"

Michael sat down, his eyes never truly leaving the door, in case it should open all by itself. Whatever it was that he had seen, it was still on the other side of that door, no matter where it might be now.

"I was woken by a loud slam of a door, don't ask me why or even how I decided to wander off but I saw something so…" He cut himself short, deciding not to describe what he really saw; what was the point of terrifying? "I saw a figure in the bedroom that was so odd-looking." He stopped to recall the figure rushing at him before continuing. "Then at the top the stairs I saw a child, then again in the dining room, where it just vanished into the wall."

Michael was feeling shattered and the night was drawing on. It was now three in the morning.

He looked straight at Sarah. "It was the nightmares before, the feeling of dread, of pain."

Sarah listened intently as Michael described what had happened, omitting only how the thing had rushed at him and he ended up like a frightened child on the floor. Michael slumped back into his chair, desperate to fall back to sleep, but he couldn't close his eyes.

The lights in the room and the newly restacked fire kept them company. Sarah was helping their father write down on paper what was now so obviously known by him. It was easier this way. Speaking was still a tiresome job for him. And if they were honest, for them too. Michael especially, although he felt guilty about it, didn't often have time for people to get their words out. He still hadn't developed the patience for such things. He sat and went over in his mind what had happened. It was now sketchy; almost like an unfinished mezzotint picture. There were flashbacks from his nightmares and he wondered if they were connected. Could these things enter someone's mind? Good luck with that one, he thought. He would have started to doubt his senses again if it wasn't for the totality of the realness, the emotions he knew to be genuine.

As daylight approached, they eventually fell asleep, finding comfort from their tiredness. It had turned nine by the time anyone had woken again. Michael took Sarah to see the footprints. Silly, he thought. Why would footprints still be there? He just assumed such a phenomenon would be respectfully waiting for him. Tentatively they returned to the upstairs bedrooms.

"It was here, sis," he said. "That feeling of dread, I became so cold… It's making my skin itch just being here."

Sarah went in front of him as they continued down the corridor and into the bedroom. It felt warm now. The sunshine was cascading in through the small window.

"Wonder what it wanted," she rhetorically asked as she looked around the room.

"I don't know," Michael replied. "But it was grotesque, hunched. Whatever it was, whatever it wanted I felt nothing but cruel intent."

After investigating the walls with inquisitive taps in a vain expectation of find answers, they left. Not wanting to stay there longer than they had to. The apparition of the young child couldn't be explained away either and no conclusion could be made about what Michael experienced. All he could state definitively was how he felt. The ordeal was now leaving him somewhat vacant; as if bereft of cognitive function. He didn't want to venture into the woods again; he felt he hadn't the energy to explore. Which suited Sarah. She wanted to spend time with their father.

CHAPTER SEVEN

It started not long after we moved in. First, we thought it was our imagination. Old place, unloved, lost grandeur and all that. We would notice little things at first. Misplaced items that we blamed each other for, or you two being silly. Even dismissed the giggles at night as imagination, but that changed. One night your mother was walking back to our bedroom when she saw this little child standing outside your room. She watched as it evaporated; it seemed to look at her before it did so. We kept it from you both, didn't want to frighten you. Besides, it didn't seem to be doing any harm.

So we carried on doing the work to the house, life stuff and taking care of you two. It seemed to settle once we had been here a little while... as if it had got used to us and the building work. I don't think it liked or understood the work. The visitations began to lessen until one night. I have to tell you now that saying I only knew of the child was not entirely true, well sort of. I never saw anything else but your mother did. It terrified her so much I now sit and wonder. She was walking across the garden to the side of the house when she had a feeling she described as not being alone. Beside her was a hooded figure. She came flying in to see me; she looked exactly how Michael looked last night. That was the only time she said anything and after that the child was seen more and more frequently. It was then that we found the area that must be the crypt, but the place just didn't feel right so we decided not to investigate. So, you see I kind of knew about the crypt being there. After which things died down a bit and eventually all that remained was us losing a pen or misplacing our glasses. I don't know why the figure is back or why you should see it last night. I'm sorry for not telling you now, all seemed stupid at the time, even more so now.

I'm used to this place, and I think this place is used to me now but you two must leave. I don't like that it's come back and seems to be attaching itself to you two. That crypt has to be buried again!

The note was penned by Sarah; spoken in broken, frustrated snatches by their father. She wandered into the dining room and sat down. It had been a labour for them both and now their father needed to rest. So did she. Sitting in silence her mind was busy processing what she had just learnt. She felt betrayed by their parents for not trusting them, even though she knew that wasn't the reason. She didn't know where Michael was. Putting the coffee pot on was probably the best way to find him, as the smell permeating the air would attract his attention. Sure enough, he soon appeared in the kitchen doorway. They were both fatigued by their nerves. Sarah showed him the note.

"Well shit!" he commented after reading it. Continuing sotto voce. "Lost his mind, superstitious…"

Sarah struck him with a glare! "I heard that! And he hasn't! God, how can you say that with everything that's been going on. Right now I'm thinking of ordering a witch doctor… and maybe he's right, maybe we should just bury that thing out there and hose the bloody place down with holy water!"

Michael looked back with an expression that suggested it was her losing their mind, not their father. Then they caught their breath. Footsteps! They could be heard quite clearly walking across the floor in the room above the kitchen.

"Oh Christ, what now!?" exclaimed Sarah.

Instead of rushing, this time they quietly stepped out of the kitchen and crept upstairs. Sarah covered her mouth to stifle a panicked gasp on hearing a playful giggle. Slowly, painfully so, they crept along the corridor to the room. The sound could still be heard. The door was shut. Michael held his breath; standing upright against the door he grasped the handle and twisted it. It seemed to take for ever. They could hear a child inside; they were sure of that. The door made no sound as it opened. To their utter astonishment something remained in the room; the misty outline of a child. They did not know how they understood it to be a child. There were no distinguishable features or any kind of form resembling a corporeal being, just a misty haze that had a presence to it. Then it was gone! No feeling of fear, no feeling of dread or pain, more the sense of a friendly encounter. Albeit unnerving.

"Well, I think it's safe to say things are getting insane," said Michael.

The day held no more for any of them. It passed with not a sound and no more visitations. It came as no relief however, for they expected something… anything to happen. They slept well enough, considering all things. As the morning broke, waking them with its rays of sun through the window, Michael was half expecting to now be visited by a spectre from Christmas past! But nothing came. No ghostly presence or noise of any kind.

This sense of peace continued for the next few days. It was unnerving in its tranquillity. They began to feel at ease, as if a huge weight was beginning to be lifted. It was strange. Two weeks later there was still nothing. The snow had stopped falling and all that was left of the ice were stubborn patches dotted about in areas of shade. Sarah had visited the village to collect essentials and together they had decided not to bury the crypt but to make it more accessible. The stairwell was now clearly visible, clean and free from all debris. The tunnel contained a purpose-built ladder than Michael had fashioned from the makeshift one he had previously constructed. There was suitable lighting and the crypt itself was clean and fully lit from the breaker in the shed. The tunnel from the crypt to the house was also clear, although they avoided using it for fear of a ceiling collapse.

Perhaps more importantly, to their subconscious minds this was the only part of the structure that still unnerved them. Michael had even installed a door frame where it entered the house, but had made sure it was still firmly boarded up and blocked. They had even booked an historical expert to come and take a look, although there would be a wait for someone to get back to them. To Michael's relief, their father seemed to be going from strength to strength and he was looking forward to returning home soon, having been away from his faithful companion far too long. He had called Mary to check in and learnt that Flint hadn't always been on his best behaviour. One morning Mary had awoken to find she had forgotten the close the door to the room where the swivel bin was kept and Flint had seized his chance. The boy always loved a bin much like his sister Dyna, who was famed in her household as a bin raider. Michael suspected it had been more than one occasion and Mary was being polite.

Each new morning at the house still brought a coldness to the air but the days were getting much warmer. Michael had even allowed his sister to use his car so that it could have a run, in preparation for his return home. Michael was looking forward to getting back to his own home, his own sanctuary. Mentally he seemed to be doing better as well, although he didn't acknowledge it; being something that was invisible to him when he was doing well but acutely painful and real when he was not.

Individually all three were still thinking about the strange occurrences that had taken place, but mostly it was at the back of their mind like some hazy Pathé newsreel, strange and distant. If it hadn't felt so real at the time, they would now be doubting themselves.

Another week passed and Sarah had grown settled. Michael had made plans to return on the following weekend. It was a Thursday morning. They would never forget the day or date.

Without any forewarning they found their father dead: he had passed away in the night. It was an emotional blow of devastating proportions. The paramedics were called but their attempts to resuscitate him were in vain. They left shortly after the doctor had attended; giving that dutiful nod of sorrow when there's nothing left to say. In view of his recent health no suspicious circumstances were recorded. The private ambulance conveyed their father away to the local hospital mortuary. It was so unreal. It made no sense. He had been getting better and seemed to have won the battle but it wasn't his stroke that killed him. It appeared that the fight had been too much for his heart.

The funeral was arranged for two weeks' time. Michael couldn't leave now. He felt numb; unable to articulate how he felt. He wasn't sure he was feeling anything. It was too difficult to understand the old man had gone. The following days Sarah cried a lot, often sporadically, sometimes being set off by a memory or an item of clothing. His bed was still how it had been left when he was taken away that morning. Neither felt able to pack it away or even touch it.

Somehow having the bed just as it was suggested he was coming back.

In the lead-up to the funeral they would often hear his voice uttering their names or calling out, as if the clocks had been turned back and they were young again. But this had nothing to do with the spooky happenings they'd experienced. They knew it was just their internal monologue voicing a comforting memory to ease the pain of someone passing.

They tried to contact people from their father's past and the small number of family members that remained alive. It wasn't entirely successful. Their father had moved about a lot in his life and though the many acquaintances he had made along the way would be saddened to know he had gone they were lost to the passing of time, friendships that enter one's life for only the briefest of moments to become just memories thereafter. Technically it should have been a large gathering but it was looking set to be a small affair.

The funeral arrangements were made and the day set for their father's final send-off and their last goodbyes. It never really is a goodbye, of course when people die; it's more of a tradition for the living to conduct on behalf of the departed. They were saying goodbye to his mortal remains, not the person they knew and loved.

The hearse left the house at ten in the morning two weeks after his death, the procession taking him through the village. Those that were about their business stopped and doffed their hats in respectful acknowledgement. There was a small wake but once it was over Michael and Sarah were left bereft and alone. Absorbed in their thoughts, the day ended in exhaustion.

Sarah didn't know what to do with herself now that Dad was gone. Looking after him had become close to all-consuming; it wasn't the fact that she had to look after him but rather that the finishing line had been taken away and she felt at a loss how to react. The prize of good health and recovery was gone and now she didn't want all the time now available to her to think about it. Michael put his energy into being as stoical as he could. He felt that was his role. It didn't, however, relieve the pain of grief.

A week had passed since the wake, when, on a Thursday, it started again. Sarah was in the kitchen. The clock on the wall read 12:15. It was after midnight. She couldn't sleep. She felt alone in her thoughts. Staring out of the window. Gazing into the void of the night. A part of her wanted to know if there was life after death. Was it life they had been witnessing coming back to the house? No matter the form? Or was it death?

That was when she saw it. As clear as if it had been walking across the grounds in the light of day. It wasn't the figure she saw originally; this time it was unmistakably a female, in a corseted crinoline dress. Her peripheral thinking read it as Victorian. She pierced the night with her eyes as she studied the figure and its movements. It was forlorn in its motion. As it came closer to the house it began to fade, eventually disappearing altogether, as if not quite making it home. It made Sarah feel a sense of sadness without knowing why.

She wasn't scared like before, although she may have been if she had known she wasn't the only one watching the figure that night. Above her in the top bedroom the hooded shape she had seen the night she called Michael was inside the house staring out of the window… watching. The lights inside the crypt that had accidentally been left on flickered and went out.

The next day was as solemn as any of the previous days since the funeral. Sarah told Michael what she had seen.

"What do you think about contacting someone to come and visit the house?" she asked.

"You mean a priest or something?"

"No, not a priest but a paranormal expert. I don't want to stay here any more, chasing answers and just waiting for the next terrifying vision, I think we need help."

She was surprised at the speed of Michael's acceptance. No sarcastic rejoinder or display of male pride to say they should keep it between them. Perhaps he was just as tired as she was and, since their father's death, he hadn't found the strength to put up any more witty counterarguments.

Later in the day they were watching TV together when they heard footsteps walking across the floor in the room above them. They looked at each other knowingly but neither was tempted to investigate this time, and they listened until the sound faded away. But this latest experience prompted them to open the laptop and go through with their task of searching for information on paranormal activities.

The browser brought up a plethora of websites and titles.

Ghost Hunter

Paranormal investigator

House cleansing of the departed

Lost souls found

Afterlife investigations

Mediums

Clairvoyants

Looking at all the images and claims was making Michael frustrated and Sarah looked like she was losing the will to live. Was it really that difficult? It was a minefield and they had no detector. Then they came across something different. No fancy website with this one. Just a brief advertisement for a team who offered to set up their equipment and conduct a scientific investigation. They looked legit, and more to the point they offered their services for free, as long as they had free access to the haunted location.

The reply to their enquiry came back the same evening; the team could come at the weekend and would like to stay for three to four days if that was acceptable. They added that they couldn't wait as Sarah's detailed description suggested an opportunity too good to miss.

CHAPTER EIGHT

Saturday dawned with a warmth in the ground that had been sorely missed for some time. In anticipation of the investigators' arrival a bed was made up, at their request, in the room where Michael had the worst of his experiences. It was ten o'clock when they arrived, pulling up in the drive in a long-wheelbase van, an estate car following behind. Three in the front of the van and two more in the car. Sarah was standing at the entrance of the house waiting to greet them after hearing the vehicles pull up.

"Morning!" said the driver, swinging the van door open. "My name's Paul." He introduced the two passengers Jane and Philip. They too got out and introduced themselves to Sarah with a cheery "Morning! Morning!"

"Good morning!" said Sarah, beginning to think that if there were any more good mornings it would soon be good evening!

The door of the car opened and out stepped a man in his fifties, Sarah surmised, somewhat older than three from the van. The gentleman almost hop skipped and jumped up to the doorway, waving his right hand in an ebullient way and carrying a portmanteau in his left.

"Hello! Good morning! Peter's the name!" he announced. Sarah took in the tweed blazer and brown brogues; she felt somehow reassured.

"Pleasure to meet you." he said, shaking Sarah vigorously by the hand. "I say, it really is exciting stuff; can't wait to get started. These are my colleagues, as you already know! And Julia will be over shortly; she's just shuffling some paperwork.".

Sarah thought the three from the van looked more akin to pop stars in comparison as she walked them through the entrance and into the hall.

"Wow!" Peter exclaimed, rubbing his hands together with excitement. "So, this is your family home you say?"

"Yes, but not our ancestral home. Our parents bought it when we were young and the condition you see it in now is thanks to their restoration efforts."

"I see. I absolutely love the vaulted ceiling as you come through, I wonder if that part actually belongs to an older building? Hmmm?" Peter replied, questioning his own thoughts.

"Perhaps. I do know the site has had many incarnations and possibly an even older settlement once stood here," said Sarah.

Peter's three colleagues stood in silence, unable to get a word in edgeways. Or just happy to let him do all the talking. Grasping his hands tightly together, Peter continued. "Well, we have the basics from you and that will do for our first night… I think we will stick to the house tonight and possibly…"

He allowed himself to be interrupted as a slight figure in round black spectacles came into the hall carrying a haversack and a clipboard.

"Hello, I'm Julia," she said in soft but pleasant tone. Sarah judged her to be in her late forties.

"I'll pop the kettle on," said Sarah and left them to get organised.

"Righto! Let's get the equipment in," Peter instructed. "We've plenty of room so we can bring it all inside and start unpacking in the hall."

When Sarah returned with a tray she was surprised by the amount of equipment they had brought with them. It looked like the backstage of a concert with several large trunks, some now open, lamps and even deck chairs. She didn't ask any questions. From what she had already seen of Peter, she thought it might just set him off. She nodded to Paul and left the tray on one side.

"Philip! Have you got the EVPs?" shouted Paul.

"Yeah, they're in the box at the back, mate, you should have the EMFs in there too."

Jane jumped off the back of the van with a box of motion detector pods. Peter was skipping about, checking off the equipment and organising where it should go. He turned to Julia with an inquisitive grin. "Anything?"

"Yes, the moment we entered the drive I felt it. This place is full to the brim, and how these poor people have coped so far is beyond me," she answered.

"Great! That's amazing!" Peter exclaimed.

Julia stepped closer, as if to whisper but without any intention to hide anything. "It's not great at all, Peter. There is something here, more than one, more than five maybe, but there is a darker presence here."

"It will be fine, Julia; we'll suss it out," he said with an attempt at a reassuring smile.

Sarah found Michael outside. Coffee in hand, leaning his forearms on the coping stones of the wall that divided the patio from the garden, looking out in reverie.

"They're here, just unloading now; you okay?" she enquired.

"Yeah, just mulling things over. I'll be in in a bit and say hello. Weird ain't it, all this."

"Maybe now we can get some answers. Come on; Mum and Dad bought this house to be our home and it's more important now than ever that we keep it that way... let's do him proud." she said, comfortingly.

Michael smiled. "Yeah, I suppose so, mate, I suppose so."

Inside they found equipment spread all over the hallway floor. Michael got the same vigorous handshake from Peter, who then introduced him to the team.

Michael and Sarah spent the day trying to keep out of the way as the team explored the house. Motion detectors were placed in every one of the upstairs rooms and one at each end of the corridors. They lit up every time Michael or Sarah forgot and kicked them flying. Peter was busying himself like a mother on Christmas Eve hanging the last of the decorations, only instead these were 'motion bells', as he liked to call them, above each doorway. The team buzzed with precise scrutiny, carefully deciding where would be the best place to take their night vision cameras.

By four o'clock everything was in place, and Michael and Sarah decided it was time to serve up a feast for their guests. Both liked to play the host and offer up good hospitality. They cooked curry for the evening meal and set it up in the dining room, avoiding the motion sensors this time.

"Ah splendid!" said Peter with his now customary enthusiasm, which they'd realised he showed to just about everything. Paul, Jane and Philip sat down with them. Julia was already at the table, quiet and pensive.

Philip started the conversation. "We're all set upstairs, everything is in place. Thought me and Paul would take the first shift in the room that you, Michael, had the… experience in."

"Splendid, splendid… capital!" enthused Peter.

"Julia and I will stay together, and Jane, would you join us?" Philip continued.

"So why is it that you don't want any more information about what's been happening?" Sarah interjected.

"Well," Peter replied, "we have what we need to spike our curiosity and, of course, to get us here in the first place." He trailed off with a haughty laugh. "But if we were to receive any more details at this time it may taint the investigation. I mean, you wouldn't want us to allow our imagination to make up the dots, and, most importantly, Julia needs to be able to relay anything she picks up back to you and Michael without you two thinking you told her about it."

"I see, well that does make sense," said Sarah.

Night hit the mansion with a heavy foreboding. The evening sky was shot through with a vein of dark red from the dying sunset until the blackness eclipsed what was left of the day. The team had split into their respective groups as agreed. Michael and Sarah felt the oppressive omnipotence that was now with them. Paul and Philip were adjusting the cameras that would watch over them and their surroundings. They were clearly feeling especially nervous, ready for what already promised to be an intimidating night. Peter, Jane and Julia were downstairs adjusting and double checking their equipment. Julia was not looking at all comfortable, even unwell. The air inside the house felt stifling. The only lights that remained on were those in the front room on the ground floor. The crackling of the fire made the only comforting sound. Michael and Sarah sat in this room; the 'base camp' as Peter had called it. If anything should happen or anyone become unnerved, they were to retreat to this room. Peter sat silently in an armchair, which was moved into the hallway for this purpose, with a notebook in one hand and a pencil in the other poised on the tip of his lips; waiting.

Jane was at the halfway point just past the first motion detector on the staircase with her legs folded against one of the steps. Again, notepad in one hand and a pencil poised. Julia was between them in the hallway. Looking, to anyone that could have seen her face, pensive. It had been decided earlier in the day that radio silence would be maintained until the first incident. Until something occurred there would be total silence. So the two groups, to all intents and purposes, were on their own, separated by the expanse of the house.

Upstairs Philip and Paul sat in the deck chairs that the group had brought with them. The door to the room was open and they had their backs to the wall. The moonlight was the only break in the darkness. They both had a clear line of vision down the corridor to the top of the stairs; beyond that, however, was left to the shadows.

In the old days of paranormal investigation there would have been large cassette players loaded with tape placed on the floor next to a flask of tea. Of course, time, as with most things, moves on. Philip and Paul had their phones plugged in with a paranormal recording app open and tins of energy drink on the floor next to their feet. Peter, downstairs, stuck with his flask of tea. Each team member had a tablet connected with the cameras that were placed around the house, so they could observe activity without the need to be in every room.

Julia was clearly feeling unwell, but this was normal under the circumstances and she was used to it. In the past she and Peter had often experienced the phenomenon and were well practised. It was Julia's responsibility to jot down whatever – or whoever – she felt and any thing or person she might connect with. Jane was there to bear witness to any phenomena that occurred and record the group's findings.

Michael and Sarah felt comforted by the company and their evident expertise, as they sat in the living room drinking their coffee and waiting. The silence felt as though it had a density to it, thick like soup.

For a while nothing happened. In their posts and positions, they waited. Jane swiped through the images on her tablet: her heart missed a beat! One of the motion detectors was going berserk! She motioned to Peter, holding up her tablet. His expression was one of utter delight. Something was happening! He crept upstairs to sit with Jane and take a closer look.

"By jove!" he whispered. "It's lit up like a seventies disco! Where is that? Which room is it?"

Jane, perhaps still pondering what a seventies disco might look like, opened up a box on the screen. "It's upstairs, top left, at the opposite end to where Philip and Paul are."

"Julia, Julia… come with me," Peter whispered loudly to get her attention, picking up his hand-held camera which illuminated his face with a green haze. They slowly walked down the corridor, edging, heel to toe, as they went.

Paul and Philip felt a pang of anxiety as they saw movement at the top of the stairs, then relaxed as they watched their colleagues disappear into the darkness.

"Okay." Peter started narrating into his microphone. "We are now walking down the top corridor of this magnificent old mansion. It is twelve thirty and we have been on watch for the last three… yes, three hours now and nothing until about ten minutes ago when Jane alerted me that one of the motion detectors had started flashing; we are now investigating."

They turned left into another corridor and saw the flickering blue, red and green light coming from the three little LEDs that were mounted on top of the detectors.

"Anything?" he asked Julia, leaning his neck in her direction.

"Yes, but I can't connect. I'm sure something is here with us but the feeling is confused," she replied.

The door to the bedroom was open, just as they had left it. In the middle of the floor was the pod. Flashing away with no obvious reason as to why.

"Something must have set it off surely?" Peter seemed to be questioning himself again.

They sat on the edge of the bed frame, against the wall under the window, looking at the open door. Then they were plunged into darkness as the flickering lights stopped. There was an icy cold that crept from the floor and circled their legs. Peter scanned the room with his camera. The lights quickly flashed once more, before stopping again.

"Something evil is in this room," said Julia. Her breath could be seen riding her words. "Something that's not meant to be here, something out of time or out of place? I can't be sure. It was... here, before the house. I feel fear, wait... it's not here. My God!" she said, turning her head to face Peter. "It's just sheer presence! The emotion of whatever stalks these rooms. But the actual being is elsewhere. I think we should leave."

"Okay, let's head back downstairs... we'll report our findings later."

Julia kept close to Peter as they headed back to the top of the stairs. Motioning to Philip and Paul who, because of the radio silence, still had no idea what was happening, they went back to the hallway, passing Jane on the stairs. All was still once more. Every now and then they swiped through the screens on their tablets but found nothing.

It was two o'clock in the morning when footsteps were heard walking across the hallway. The sound was unmistakable. They were getting louder and to their amazement something was being picked up on the camera, moving across the floor and heading straight towards them. A figure could just about be imagined from the hazy image. Jane, isolated on the stairs, was filled with fear. Peter was trembling with excitement and barely able to contain himself. The outline on the camera stopped, and so did the footsteps. They then sounded again but at a faster pace… heading towards the blocked entrance to the tunnel. The figure was gone and once more silence fell. Peter scribbled his notes, lit by his pocket torch.

Tiredness, even to a team that was used to it, still came as a struggle at around three thirty and heavy eyelids were the new occurrence to watch out for. Julia wasn't picking up anything and nothing was being triggered on the cameras or motion pods. Paul and Philip were struggling to stay awake, the long drive to the house taking its toll. The energy drinks were now just empty cans and the supply was downstairs. They didn't want to move for fear of ruining the investigation, but Paul had to visit the bathroom. The house was in complete darkness when he decided to go in search for the toilet, giving a hitchhiker's thumb to Philip to let him know where he was off to. They had become used to each other's signals. He had left it too long and his bladder became an agonising pressure point with every step, so that it was pretty much all he could think about. Philip, who had fallen into a deep sleep and missed the signal, was pricked into consciousness by the creaking of floorboards. Expecting Paul to be there, he turned around. But where Paul should have been was a sinister, hunched figure, hooded. Philip froze with fear. He had never had such an experience before. He had become brave, even cocky after so many nights on lookout, but his confidence was shattered now. He was petrified. All alone with this figure. It seemed to be hovering and at the same time firmly planted to the floor. He was transfixed by the face; gaunt and despairing. The hurt, at least the emotion of hurt, was all-consuming. Philip felt pain, hunger and loss. An ache in his very soul. He wept; tears rolled down his cheeks. The figure's face was horrible, the essence of horror. The room had become icy cold with the thing's presence. Philip tried to let out a scream, shout, but he couldn't. He couldn't even move. Then he noticed the smell... the stench of death. Philip had seen death before; he had smelt it. But this was the very origin of death and decay, the wretched and unwanted depths of hell. A primeval rot.

The figure sunk back, as if deflating into the fabric of the bedroom, leaving Philip on his own once more, but forever changed by the experience. He stared out from the bedroom where the figure had stood, not daring to close his eyes again, in case that would cause the figure to return. Paul had been gone an age, where was he? Philip yearned for his friend's return; he wasn't sure how long he could go on being alone. His cockiness had been taken away from him, his courage stolen. He felt violated by the creature that had imposed its presence on him.

His heart jumped into his throat when lights started flashing in the corridor until he realised it was his colleague setting them off on his return from the bathroom.

"Christ," said Philip in a hushed voice. "Looks like you've seen a ghost!".

"You piece of shit," Philip replied through gritted teeth.

"Alright, mate, what's got into you? Number one turned into a number two. You try having a shit in the dark in a haunted house, for fuck's sake."

"You and your fucking arse!" Philip's eyes glared into Paul's as he grabbed hold of his arm.

"Fuck me. You really have seen something, ain't ya, mate." Paul's tone was more conciliatory now.

"It was something terrible, mate, I don't know how to explain it. It was…" Philip stopped, buried his head into Pauls shoulders and began to sob. It was a cry that felt unnatural; not of him, not really.

"That's it, mate," Paul declared. "We're calling it a night. Let's go get the others."

As they left the room, Philip knew he would never return to it. Lights blazed at the flip of every switch as Paul called an end to the night's proceedings.

"What the blazes!" Peter demanded an explanation.

"Sorry, Peter, but that's it for the night; we'll explain later." Peter knew Paul wasn't one to give up, and respecting the authority in his voice he accepted the succinct answer and knew better than to prod further. Besides, his own internal excited child assumed it was for a very good, paranormal reason.

CHAPTER NINE

It was four thirty when proceedings were finally halted. The usual procedure was now followed. A quick debrief from the General (Peter) then try to get their heads down for a few hours before the day started in earnest. They hadn't disturbed Michael and Sarah but had set up camp in the dining room, where they rested soundly until the first of them woke at nine thirty to the smell of bacon and – a quick sniff to confirm suspicions – sausages and quite possibly fried bread. Paul was certain of it. He adored fried breakfast, something he was soon to find he had in common with his host.

Michael stood at the hob, spatula in hand, prodding the food in the frying pan. Sarah had laid the table and now flitted from cupboard to table with condiments. She looked up.

"Morning, Paul, hope you all like a good breakfast… any vegies in your group?"

Michael looked round. "Morning, Paul."

Paul's tiredness was already dissipating at the prospect of shortly having a full belly. He sat down from the implied invitation and was soon joined by the rest of the team. As they discussed the night Julia stayed monosyllabic. She felt hurt that she hadn't in any way connected with the most terrifying incident. In fact, she had been blissfully unaware it was taking place. She was worried that her colleagues would now think her unimportant, incompetent or a worthless fraud. Julia had always suffered from self-doubt and now it seemed that the spirit world may have the same opinion.

It was decided that the team now needed to know everything. The house had proved its worth to them and they needed to put a plan together. After all, they were investigators, not ghostbusters. The feeling that the thing Philip had experienced was more akin to an actual creature than some ghostly apparition struck a chord with Michael and Sarah, who ran in detail through their own experiences and showed the team the paperwork belonging to the house, and told them what Sid had recounted to Michael. When the name Tolhurst was mentioned, Julia ushered the group to silence.

"He is here, now... standing quite calmly, looking straight ahead," she said.

"Where?" asked Sarah, looking around.

"Over by that window, out in the corridor. I've not sensed him before. He is a new presence. Why only now I don't know. I feel control with this one. He likes to be in control. He built this house, I think. He's walking away... he's gone now." Julia relaxed her gaze.

Michael looked on. Not long ago he would never have believed such rubbish but now it all seemed perfectly reasonable.

"Excellent!" shouted Peter, creating a general jerk of surprise with the sudden interjection.

Sarah wanted to know more. "Anything else?"

"Nothing else," said Julia, "but I'm sure I will sense him again… it's difficult to know how heavy a presence he is." After a short pause, she continued. "You see, sometimes all that you are left with is an imprint in time, like a glass shadow, if you get my meaning. The image of the person is there but they are no longer with us. Then you get the trapped spirit; they know they are here and, well, some like hanging around, some don't! This one was a little unusual in that I couldn't pick up what he was. But that sometimes happens and eventually I find out. Then of course you get the bad spirits; no one wants them in their house… and that's when we get to your experience; and yours, Philip. I have to tell you and Michael that there is something far worse here, something terrifying, something I have never felt but know all too well to be evil. I felt a dark presence here when we arrived. It eclipsed all the others."

Michael stopped her in her tracks. "That sounds really ominous. And others?"

"Yes, it is as you say ominous and yes, there are others. You have more than one, two, three… I believe possibly many spirits in this house. Some have been here a long time, others are a little newer. They are gradually making themselves known to me… only time will tell."

"Right," said Peter in an uncharacteristically quieter tone. "Let's discuss our notes and get ready for tonight."

Throughout the day they adjusted their equipment and double-checked connections. The prospect of the night ahead was all the more exciting now that they had been told all about the tunnel, the crypt and the sightings made by Sarah and Michael, and in consequence had decided to open up the blocked entrance. Peter enthusiastically volunteered to stake out the crypt. Feeling it wasn't right for him to be left alone Michael volunteered to be with him, dismissing the objections of some of the team. Sarah decided she would like to stay with Julia. She and her brother were now honorary investigators!

This time round Jane would join Paul and Philip in the dining room and hall. All was agreed and finalised by four that afternoon, so as there wasn't much left to do before night fell they sat playing a board game and enjoying each other's company. Quite forgetting the time. Sarah and Michael felt a sense of relief, enjoying the laughter and growing familiarity and forgetting their recent grief for the moment.

"Good God!" Peter exclaimed. "Look at the time; we must get into position. Well, Michael and I at the very least!" Sarah couldn't help notice the juxtaposition between old and new. Peter pulling out his phone to check the time reminded her of a member of the landed gentry inspecting his pocket watch, showing displeasure that the dinner gong was running behind schedule. Seeing him now she thought Peter would suit a pocket watch better than its modern counterpart. It struck her how time repeats itself; the humble pocket watch replaced by the wristwatch but now replaced by a timepiece being pulled from a pocket again.

The shuffle and movement of people brought Sarah out of her brief reverie. Deck chairs had been placed in the crypt earlier in the day along with a portable heater. Flasks were now filled and double layers of clothing donned. Radios working? Check. Tablets? Check. It was time to go. Sarah watched from the window as they disappeared into the wooded area. It had been agreed that on this night no one would go upstairs, and they would concentrate on the rooms at ground level. This was partly to have respite from the nerves that would be induced should their phantom come back – the word phantom had come up at breakfast and seemed to have stuck – and partly to know if it was confined to certain areas. They waited.

It was now, according to the display on the tablet, 21:00. An hour passed, and nothing other than the passing of time had occurred. 23:00 was now illuminated on the screen and still nothing. Philip took a sip of his energy drink. Tiredness was setting in early.

00:05 starred back at them as they clock watched, wondering whether it was time to change position. Julia took a second walk over to the tunnel entrance, wondering how the two in the crypt were getting on. The signal to their tablet had been unsteady but Peter had instructed that they, he and Michael were to remain a standalone unit in the crypt should the connection fail. No communications other than the radio. A breakdown in Wi-Fi was expected due to the location and the risks accepted. Julia, never leaving the eyeline of her group, felt nothing. The house was literally silent to her.

One o'clock in the morning now passed on the hands of the clock in the hallway. Time slowed. Jane gazed at her tablet. The time read 01:28. The sound of a door groaning under its own weight as it slowly moved. Or more to the point was slowly pushed.

This was it! Their ears pricked; it was beginning!

Jane scrolled through her tablet; nothing yet. The house lay in silence once more but it felt very different now. They knew something had arrived in the darkness and was now with them in that great house. The darkness seemed to get even darker. Julia began lighting some of the candles that she had placed around each room. It was something she did, preferring the older traditions than relying entirely on modern technology.

The candles flickered, stood burning, then flickered again. Hearts had a faster beat than previously. There was a faint sound of laughter, barely audible. A child's playful giggle. Sarah, who had followed Julia into the hall, looked down at her feet.

Whispering, she grabbed hold of Julia's arm. "Look!"

There were newly laid, glistening wet footprints on the floor. Small, closely spaced, like those of a child. Leading away from them, towards and up the staircase. The team realised the prints were heading away from the darkness… the giggles stopped. Sarah was compelled to follow. Julia, about to join her, suddenly stood still. She could feel a malign presence that was making itself known. Anger with them. A hurt ego of enormous magnitude.

Sarah had kept her focus on the footprints, building her own courage to keep track of them. She was halfway up the staircase, just before it turned onto the first landing, when a heavy chair from the hallway screeched across the floor and hit hard into the wall as if it had been thrown.

"LEAVE!"

A command from a disembodied voice. Sarah let out a high-pitched screech as she ran down the stairs and headed for the door, where the others were already waiting. No one seemed to know why or where they were going.

"Bloody hell!" Philip shouted.

"Well, we've never heard voices before," said Sarah.

After a few minutes they tentatively stepped back inside the hall. The chair was still where it had landed. Nothing else so far. Unbeknown to them there was a shadow watching. Had anyone looked, the reflection could be seen in the face of the clock. But no one could see from where they were standing.

Julia's nerves were shaking; she had never heard such a voice before either, but she didn't want to admit that to the group. Voice or not, however, she could still sense the presence. The silence was broken by a loud bang, but from where or what they didn't know.

"OH MY FUCKING DAYS!" Philip shouted out.

"Yeah, second that, mate." Paul concurred, for the time being holding his nerve a little better.

Looking to one another for courage, very slowly they began to walk towards where they thought the noise was coming from. BANG! A pause, each unknowingly checking the others were still with them. If one had broken ranks, they would surely all have fled. Their nerves were as delicate as crystal balancing on a spinning plate. The house was dark. Another bang. The sound was slightly less this time. Bang. It was getting more subdued. Bang, bang, bang. Turning the corner into the kitchen Sarah could see that the door of one of the units was slamming shut. That wasn't the most unnerving aspect, however; it was the evident fact that something was opening it again, then slamming it closed with force. It meant only one thing. Although they could see no one, they were in effect looking directly at whatever it was that was doing it. Twice more the cupboard slammed. Sarah felt an ice-cold breeze pass her, followed by an intense searing heat to her face which caused her to scream out loud. As her companions comforted her, Sarah reflected that the night had certainly started with a bang, and wondered what else might happen.

"So, this is a little boring! But excellent company, old chap!" Peter suddenly announced, out of the silence that filled the crypt.

Michael was startled out of his daydream. "Depends on your point of view I guess, Peter. I was wondering how the others were getting on." He shuffled in his deckchair to get comfortable.

"Hopefully a little more action that we're getting down here, eh?"

Michael had been amused from the start by Peter's unwavering confidence and nerve. He wondered if it was all a front or if this man really believed in the supernatural. He'd learnt that such supreme confidence is sometimes born out of ignorance or not believing in the reality of a situation.

"Peter? I've been wondering what it is that makes you the way you are?"

There was a little of the rhetorical about Michael's question, but there was no hesitation in the reply. "Ha! Ha! I like you Michael. Most people just think I'm a bit odd, but you just come out and ask. I like that. You see, I've never really suffered with depression, apart from this one time that took the legs from under me I don't mind telling you, but since then nothing really matters. Maybe that's a sign of depression, who knows but the fact is we're all just on a big ball hurtling through space around a bigger ball of fire, and when you see the bigger picture, well, sat here waiting for a ghost, I reckon we can face up to that!"

Michael couldn't argue with logic like that. He quietly took a sip of his tea. Apart from where they actually were it felt much like a night fishing trip, waiting for a bite. They had placed the chairs midway between the entrance from the slope and the tunnel. It was cold but their prudent preparations were keeping them comfortable. Peter still had a smear of mud down one leg after losing his grip when descending. Michael did all he could to control a rumbling outburst of laughter but every now and then that image still prodded him, daring him to laugh out loud.

Back at the house, the others had left the kitchen and assembled in the front room. Paul once again had to submit to his movements and go to the toilet; only this time a flower pot outside was preferable to anywhere inside the house, least of all the upstairs bathroom on his own. His return was met by the sound of motion bells ringing. Sarah cautiously set off to find out which doorway it was. Carefully opening the door she walked slowly, nervously out into the hall.

Standing at the top of the stairs was the figure of a woman. No longer of this world, this ghostly apparition now presented herself for the first time. Never seen or indeed felt before. She stood on the penultimate step, a terrifying image. Sarah looked on; her throat dry. The woman's head turned as if in acknowledgement of Sarah. Her eyes were sunk into her face; dark and pitiful. Her lips were thin and drawn in at the mouth. Her gaze now set like stone on Sarah, she began to descend the stairs, her dress appearing to drape on each step as she glided down. This figure was not the one Sarah had seen in the grounds.

As the others came out into the hallway to find out what was happening, the woman's eyes seemed to absorb their presence and judge their existence. From the blackness of this figure Sarah could see the spectre of a hand. It was gaunt and pale, more bone than flesh. The forefinger was fidgeting with a chatelaine. The figure took on a more and more solid appearance as it approached the group. No one moved. It clearly knew they were there and it was acting in a way that was self-aware. It turned to face the entrance and walked towards the door. Before leaving, it looked over once more to the group and motioned its head towards the tunnel. The hand began to rise in an outward gesture before the entire figure disintegrated into a cloud of mist.

What was this new apparition, Sarah wondered. Why would it show itself now? What might have brought it out from its dark hiding place? Moments after it disappeared the faint sound of a child's laughter was heard again, trailing off into the distance of the house. There was a collective sigh of relief as the team felt the manifestation was over. They instinctively looked at Julia.

"That was a very powerful entity," she said. "And so much pain accompanied her. Such dreadful pain. I've never felt dormant suffering suddenly come to life like that. I'm certain, now that she has shown herself, we will hear from her again."

Standing there, at the foot of the stairs, Sarah inexplicably felt that she was a part of what had just happened, and sensed that the others were feeling it too. They returned to the room, quite forgetting that it was the motion sensors that had alerted them in the first place. But it wasn't the woman on the stairs that had set them off. She had distracted them.

"As amazing as this place is, I'm getting close to losing my arsehole," Paul announced, though no one in the group had shown any inclination to know how his backside was holding up.

Sarah didn't say a word. She was deep in thought about the gesture the woman had made towards the tunnel.

CHAPTER TEN

The night had passed peacefully for the two in the crypt. Looking through the footage and analysing the recording apps came to nothing. The only thing the sensors had picked up that night was the visiting fox. The same one that had found the kindly gesture Michael had placed by the outbuilding at the height of the snowfall.

The house, however, proved a box of delights for Peter. He was almost fixated, like a panther when it has finished stalking and is about to pounce. Hanging on every word, every detail he could absorb from what the group had to disclose.

He finally sat back. "Well, bless my soul! Incredible, just incredible!"

All were tired but the night's work was extending far into the day with no time to rest. Julia had drawn up a mind map that covered the table in the dining room. Sightings, times, days and dates were recorded, along with descriptions of each sighting, a growing list.

Michael went outside to drink his coffee. He needed some quiet time to think things through. Never in his wildest imaginings would he have thought he'd be in such a situation. He needed to be alone; he did like his own company and as much as the team fascinated him, his social reserves had been depleted and sipping his coffee outside in the cold air was providing a well-needed top-up for his resilience. He was missing his dad and he was missing Flint. He could do with a cuddle from his old mate right about now; he'd often found the greatest comfort in the company of animals. He sat on the stone steps, gazed out across the land and breathed in the surroundings, absorbing nature's spirit. He had just reached the bottom of the cup and was gazing absent-mindedly at the ring of coffee that was left when his thoughts was interrupted by Sarah

"Wondered where you went; all your life you've liked to go missing," she said with a knowing smile as she sat down beside him. "You alright?"

Michael gave a thoughtful look as if he wanted to want to tell her something. But in the end he just answered, "Yeah, let's go back in."

The day was already busy with preparations for another night. When they could they slept, often through exhaustion rather than willingness. The house was filled with the aroma of coffee; it was as if it was on a non-stop pipeline from the kitchen. This night they would swap roles. Philip, who was beginning to argue they already had enough information to be going on with, was allocated the crypt and Peter would brook no argument from him. With him would be Jane and Julia. Michael would stay with Paul in the upper levels of the house this time while Peter volunteered for the hall, hoping for an opportunity to meet the lady of the stairs as he had christened her.

127

"Righto lads, good hunting." Peter's words were a strong hint that it was time to get started. As they set off up the stairs Peter made himself at home on the chair that had been thrown across the hall, deliberately choosing it for that very reason. From where he now sat, he had an excellent vantage point and watched Paul and Michael disappear into the top corridor. The lights were on until everyone had checked in. Peter was quite content with his tea and blanket across his legs, one of the tablets balanced on his lap.

The walkie talkie crackled. "All set here, we're all good and ready." It was Sarah, who'd volunteered to join the crypt detachment after being quite forgotten in the planning.

"Good, good," acknowledged Peter. "All set upstairs?" he inquired.

Michael's response came crackling back. "Yeah all good, we're set up in the attic, didn't want to bother you earlier but we thought we heard something so we're taking a look."

"There you go." Philip poured piping hot tea from the flask into Jane and Julia's mugs. He was surprised how warm they were considering the environment they were in. Sarah was already savouring her hot chocolate.

"Feel anything?" he asked Julia.

"No, oddly not, feels creepy down here but nothing paranormal."

The next half hour was spent talking about their favourite films, if only to break the silence, before moving onto a vain attempt at a decent game of I-spy. It was a weird situation. To be sitting in such a strange place and still not have a thing happen to them. It was eleven o'clock. As they chatted and giggled their minds drifted from their task. Outside, the woods rustled in the deep darkness. No animals were present; none would have dared to be. Nature has a sense for such things, things that manifest from the dark evolution unique to the human condition. There was a malaise that now enveloped the woods and around the top of the crypt, enclosing all that lay before it and suffocating the land, placing the stairs to the entrance in total darkness. The lights in the shaft went out.

It was a smell of cloth. Fabric that was coarse and old, moving gently. Brushing at the senses. The smell was an ancient one and Peter's senses struggled to connect it all together. He had fallen asleep, slumped in his chair. As he slowly came too, he found his line of sight obscured. He moved his head from side to side as his senses became clearer, instinctively raised his hand to brush something away from his face but connected with something solid. Someone's ankle, he recognised the shape of the fibula, and suddenly he was fully awake.

He looked up. In front of him was the figure of the woman, her housekeeper's keys around her waist. She had come to make her presence felt; of that he was certain. He shuddered as he took in the sight that met his eyes. Before him hung this figure of a woman, gaunt and pale, dangling from a rope that ascending into the darkness of the hallway ceiling. Unable to move, Peter sat there aghast, his instinctive delight mixed with the trepidation that was sapping his energy. 'My God!' he whispered. He gently pushed back against his chair and looked up at her. He felt only pity for this thing that hung before him. The eyes sunk into its face. The entire body lifeless. He averted his gaze to see where his tablet was. When he looked back the figure had vanished, leaving only an icy feeling through Peter's veins. All around him was darkness and cold. The hairs on the back of his neck tingled, sending an unnerving paralysis to his head. It was deafeningly silent. Regaining his senses he looked around him. He was scared. Scared to move but still delighted. Nevertheless, Peter didn't like being scared; it scared him.

He made to get up, then stopped himself. At the far end of the hall he was sure he could make out the figure again. Tall, dressed in black and walking across towards the entrance of the tunnel. To Peter it looked as though she was going through the motions of unlocking a door, but she was too far away from where the actual door was. Another few steps forward and she was gone. The faint sound of giggles could be heard again. Now Peter got up with torch in hand and slowly walked to where he saw she had been. There was nothing to witness, his own frightened imagination was taking hold and he felt uncharacteristically nervous. He was all alone in the darkness and for the first time in a very long time Peter rushed to a light switch and turned it on, immediately regretting it and damning himself for being so susceptible to fear and his own imagination.

"Bugger it."

With the light on, the atmosphere took on the feel of a mortuary. Even the wood looked cold as stone. He decided to go make himself a cup of tea; the normality of a mundane task would ease his anxieties. Even Peter felt vulnerable sometimes. Thumbling for another light switch in the kitchen he tripped and only just saved himself from a complete fall by bracing himself against the table.

"For pity's sake, Peter, sort yourself out, man," he said to himself through gritted teeth. Sometimes the only person who could frustrate Peter was Peter.

Peter momentarily lost his thoughts while he stirred his tea. Looking up he gazed out of the window and thought about the figure that had been seen. He looked over to the wooded area and wondered if the rest of the group had already got a story of their own to tell. It was still dark with plenty more possibilities but already he couldn't wait to recount his own experience. As he looked, he could see a darkness that was somehow denser than the night that surrounded it, but didn't make any connection and turned to make his way back to his chair. He stood still; the chair had moved and was now pointing towards one of the rooms. He walked towards the chair, only to witness it shunt slightly on its feet. Something was moving it. He took a few more steps. It dragged more loudly this time, moving more sharply than before. Peter took a sip of his tea and watched, not moving an inch. The light that he'd left on in the kitchen went out; what was especially unnerving was the sound of the switch being clicked.

There was a coldness like he'd never felt before, and though he was standing in total darkness now, he could see his breath. His body gave out all the ancient signals that evolution had provided that he was in danger. Peter started to concentrate; deliberately putting his emotions in check, an endeavour that quickly became redundant. To his left side he could feel her again. A heavy presence. It was unmistakable that someone was there. With just a slight movement of the eyes he saw her come into the periphery of his vision. The dread and excitement of such an experience made his heart thump. Once again Peter was feeling the effects of fear. He could tell she was looking straight ahead but he somehow knew that she was completely aware of his presence. Peter surmised from her clothing that her physical life would have been in a period before the Victorian. Something about the smell of her clothing triggered a memory that he couldn't quite place. An experience he had or something he'd read in the past put her somewhere in the Georgian era.

Her sheer presence was weighing on him more and more heavily. The burden of her very soul was casting an outstretched shadow into the dark hall. She moved forward, and now with her back to Peter she moved towards the chair. She stopped, turned her head and starred straight at him. Her features were unclear but a face could still be made out around those sunken eyes. Her head stayed fixed as her body pivoted. Within that same movement her entire body glided backwards before disappearing once more.

For a time, the coldness remained before lifting completely. Peter stayed rooted. He sipped his tea. It was the only thing he could do to prove he could still move.

None of this was known to the two upstairs who had heard only footsteps stalking the corridor. The light being turned on had not reached far enough to interrupt their night. Usually, footsteps would be a terrifying experience on their own, but in the circumstances they almost discounted them in trepidation over what might yet come. They sat and waited to see if anything would appear. Eventually they heard a terrifying groan from the darkened corridor; it was enough to make the two recoil into themselves.

"Shit" Paul whispered. "I take it you heard that?"

"Yes, I did that," Michael replied, in an equally hushed tone.

The sound came again, so haunting that it hit every nerve. Paul turned on the night vision and as quietly as he could began narrating what he saw.

"We have just heard what we think is a voice in one of the corridors at the very top of the house. It has a terrifying tone. I'm with Michael and we are about to take a look."

From toe to heel they edged along the corridor, illuminated only by the night camera. It was especially nerve-racking passing the rooms that still had their doors open, the dark voids only adding to the already unsettling atmosphere. Paul placed an EVP detector on the floor in the hope of catching any further sounds. Even in this state of anxiety Michael couldn't get over the fact they never seem to run out of the damn things.

They continued along the corridor; none of the sensors had been activated, which suggested no unseen movement, but they knew they weren't alone. Then the horrible groan was there again, this time ascending in volume. As they froze the sensors lit up in a cacophony of colours before they felt a force charging towards them and shoving them aside.

As suddenly as it had all started the phenomena stopped. The atmosphere relaxed. They were left alone and terrified. But the recording equipment had done its job.

In the crypt, the four watchers were unaware of the dark stillness that now lay above them or the extinguished lights in the shaft. Before they understood what was happening all the other lights went out. A mysterious energy was creeping its way along the floor of the crypt, circling itself around their ankles and striking an icy stab into their bodies.

Julia had felt this before. In the blackness she alone knew what was with them. The presence she had felt, with Peter, in that bedroom was with them now, in the darkness of the crypt. This time, however, Julia sensed a consciousness. She sat in the darkness and tried to focus on what might happen next.

Sarah's hand was combing the floor looking for the torch that had fallen from her lap. Finding it, she fumbled with the button, desperate to get some light, and darted the beam around the walls. The darkness had felt overwhelming, grabbing hold of them in a tight embrace.

This phenomenon was tightening its grip on Julia. "I can't breathe," she gasped. "It's horrendous. Oh my God!"

Sarah could see the life draining from Julia's eyes as she shone the torch on her face.

"What is it?" she asked

Philip was trying to get his night camera working. They'd been so relaxed, chatting and subconsciously thinking nothing would happen because the house had been the focus of activity that they had neglected to be ready to react. He felt something like a hand grab his side. He shouted and leapt up from his chair. A flash of the torch caught a strange figure darting across the room, as if trying to escape the beam. Whatever it was it preferred the darkness. One of the chairs was picked up and thrown against the wall, smashing to pieces, and in the confusion Philip felt one of the broken chair legs strike him across the face, bloodying one of his eyes. He screamed as he backed away, finding himself near the exit, but the doorway was blocked by some unknown force that pushed him to the floor.

"Philip!" Jane shouted out, seeing him fall through the intermittent light from her torch.

Sarah was holding her nerve but only just, and shone her torch towards the small tunnel that led back to the house. "Let's get of here, before anyone else gets hurt!"

"No, not the tunnel!" Julia cried out, but her entreaties were ignored in the desperation to escape.

Sarah went first, scrambling across the floor with torch in hand. Philp forced Julia through behind Sarah, then made way for Jane. He too held a torch tightly in his hand. As he left, the light flashed across the crypt. He would never forget what he saw.

Peter was inspecting the chair that had moved using his own small torch. He had his second fright of the night when the door to the tunnel was kicked open.

"What the blazes!"

"Quick, turn the lights on, get the lights on!" shouted Sarah, with no time for pleasantries.

The other three burst out into the hall. Mumbling and out of breath. Philip turned sharply to peer into the dark opening. Nothing was coming. Not yet anyway. Julia ran forward and pushed hard against the broken door as Paul and Michael came running down to see what was happening.

No one asked, no one hesitated, they all followed. Out into the darkness of the night, stopping by the parked vehicles. Julia looked drained and sick, like a child of whom anxiety had taken complete hold on their first day of school and there wasn't anything anyone could do for her. Peter grabbed hold of her and held her tight. What exactly was going on? Only Julia would be able to offer an explanation. Philip looked skittish; his eyes darting as if he was expecting someone to join them. Paul sat down on the ground, where Michael joined him as they watched Julia and Peter, waiting for an answer. Sarah was in shock too and sat down next to Jane on the edge of one of the large stone flowerpots that adorned the front of the house.

Eventually Julia was able to compose herself but she clearly wasn't prepared to go back into the house.

"Go on," Peter gently encouraged her.

"I know what stalks this place now," she began. "It was the very thing that presented its presence to us in the upstairs bedroom, Peter. The presence was dark enough and scared me because of the sheer malevolence of it. But tonight it showed itself to me in all its horror and I instantly saw what it was. There are absolutely others here too. Some in pain and some I'm sure that still haven't presented themselves. But this is the one they fear and they dare not tread when it decides to make an appearance.

"It's the darkest of souls. The oldest entity that resides within these grounds. Before the house was built. On occasions it has been latent, some kind of resting menace. It is so old that I believe it has been here for a thousand years or more. It's trapped here, but make no mistake; this is it's domain. It is in charge. Something happened to it. To cause such hate and suffering. It felt like it had climbed inside and was crushing my heart. There is more to learn…"

She looked at Peter.

"But I don't know if I have the strength. It's something I have never dealt with. All I know is I want to be away from here right now. I'm sorry but it's too powerful for me, I need to gather my strength. Do you know of a place I can stay in the village, Sarah?"

Michael looked at the shocked faces; they all were feeling the effects of the last few hours. But he could sense that the younger ones felt it a little disloyal that one of the team would want to abandon them. Yet they surely understood that for a psychic the experience must be even more acute than it was to them.

As the morning of the new day began to spread its light the group were to their own surprise still in much the same position they were when they fled the house. The night before was all starting to seem very diluted now.

"There's a couple of B&B's that I'm sure will have room, if you still want to, Julia?"

"Yes, thank you." She looked up at the house as if in anticipation of it mocking her.

"You sure you're okay now?" asked Michael as he pushed the gear leaver into fourth.

"Yes, I'm okay," answered Julia. "But you all must take great care, and don't for one minute think that place is your home any more. Peter will contact someone we know, who's far more experienced in matters like these."

She slumped to her left with her head leaning against the window and gazed out. Michael guessed it was a good time to leave it at that. By now he thought nothing could surprise him. What had started with an early-morning phone call all those weeks ago had now totally and utterly changed his perspective on reality and the predetermined set of rules he thought the world worked by.

Back at the house the rest of the group tentatively gathered together in the dining room. They all went together when making drinks in the kitchen. So none of them were left alone. They felt that a ghostly apparition could present itself at any opportune moment if it so wished. It was as if the rules between the two worlds had been broken. Even Peter felt they were losing ground to an overwhelming enemy force. But he wanted to stay longer, as perhaps the ground could be recovered.

"I need to say something," said Philip as they sat around the table, the aroma of freshly brewed coffee pot filling the room. "When we entered the tunnel and I flashed the torch ahead, what I saw terrified me. I didn't want to say anything before. I think we were all a bit on edge to say the least. But I think I saw what Julia felt. It was like the thing I saw in the bedroom only fully manifested… properly, if that makes sense."

He poured himself more coffee. "I felt the presence more than I saw it. But what I saw was no less horrifying. I thought it was going to grab me and pull me back. I have never been so scared to be at the back of a queue. It was hunched yet it filled the entire room. The eyes were unblinking, staring straight at me. It seemed to emerge from that darkness with a new depth of blackness all of its own."

He looked up from his coffee, to see if everyone was paying attention. They were.

"I could see its face but can't describe what I saw now. That face is still with me but I can't, I just can't describe it. I felt certain it wanted to keep us there. I don't want to know why. It felt like a vampire, robbed of its prey."

"A vampire!?' It almost sounded mocking when Paul said it out loud after an uncomfortable pause.

Philip's face reddened.

"Sorry mate," Paul went on. "Didn't mean it to come out like that but we're here for an odd sound of footsteps or a ghostly white lady poking about, not all this bollocks! It's bloody mad." He reached for the coffee pot. "What say you, Sarah?"

She had her elbows on the table, supporting her head. Making circular motions with her forefingers on her temples. "I don't know, after all this time and everything that has gone on, I never thought it could be this bad. I mean, where do we go from here?"

Paul looked at Peter. "Well, I don't want to stir the shit but we've got the recordings to listen to from last night. To think Michael and I thought we were having it rough!"

They pulled the chairs closer together to listen. Paul pressed play. Seconds passed and it was starting to sound like nothing had been picked up. Then the same terrifying voice sounded, but this time words could be made out.

"Your turn, your turn, your turn."

The repetition was not a pleasant listening experience. But what did it mean? It made no sense.

"Fascinating, just fascinating." Peter's eyes were aglow with questions. "You know, I thought I was having all the fun but then I heard the sounds upstairs."

"You heard it too?" Philip asked as he and Paul looked at Peter with evident surprise.

"I did indeed."

Sarah was distracted by her thoughts arising from the recording on the tape, so in an attempt to break the spell she asked, "So, what about you Peter? How was your night? What were you doing with that chair?"

"Well, when all this was going on, I had a visit from that housekeeper woman. In fact, rather embarrassingly, I fell asleep and I awoke to find this lady hanging. Right in front of me actually. That was my first experience; after that she appeared again before vanishing. The chair, well, that moved of its own accord. I was still investigating when you burst in."

"Hanging?" Sarah wanted confirmation.

"Yes, my dear, it was quite remarkable."

Michael found a B&B for Julia, and although it was rather a basic affair she was already looking far more relaxed. Michael decided to stay with her for a little while and they drank tea in the parlour.

"So what do you think is really going on in our house?"

"Your house has problems of its own, Michael. And the ground it sits on has far more history to it than anyone is ever likely to know. I don't suppose anything was documented from the thing I felt. Stuff like that are where spooky woods and haunted forests are born, passed down through the ages from a time when people couldn't understand what they were experiencing.

"Hence why we all grow up with a feeling of 'don't go in there' or 'that place is cursed'; its left over from old coping mechanisms."

"Well, if you're okay I'll leave you be. When do you think you'll be back up?"

"I'll keep in contact with Peter, and once we've arranged some help I'll rejoin you. I'm sorry, Michael." She bowed her head as if embarrassed by her actions.

"No need to apologise, Julia. I think we're all on our last nerve right now and you must be more so than us. I'll see you soon."

Michael took his time on the way home. It was nice to be alone briefly with his own thoughts. One thought kept prodding him. It's not your home any more, that's what Julia had said. This whole thing was getting beyond his grasp but he still had no idea how to deal with it. He needed his friend. He propped his phone on the centre console and phoned Mary.

"Hello?" The old familiar voice was comforting.

"Mary? Hello, its Michael. It's nice to hear you," he said.

"Oh, hello my dear, how are you?"

"I've been better, Mary, but that's a story for another time. More important, how are you? I really am so sorry to have left you with Flint for so long."

"Oh that's quite alright, my dear, I've loved the company, he's been a lovely companion for me. Would you like to talk to him?"

"You must have read my mind, Mary." Michael adjusted himself in his seat with childlike excitement. He could hear Mary's voice trail off as she went to find the dog.

"Flint, Flint, come 'ere, Flint, look. No, Flint, look, no… Flint, come 'ere, what have I got, look."

It was just what Michael needed; he was chuckling away to himself imagining his faithful companion looking the wrong way and wondering what the hell Mary was going on about. Then there was a loud bark, then another. Evidently Flint had finally walked up to the mouthpiece.

"Thank you, Mary, I'd give anything to have him by my side again. Still, I'm hoping soon." There was genuine delight in his voice.

"That's quite alright my dear, you off again now?"

"Yes, afraid so, and thanks again, Mary."

"No problem, take your time, all the best."

And with that the phone was silent again. Just as the house came into view.

"How's Julia?" asked Sarah when Michael found them in the dining room.

"She's okay now, still a bit agitated though." He was anxious to find out about this other person who would be able to help.

"Ah yes, I must go make that phone call," said Peter when he asked. "Lovely woman. Let's hope she's available."

Michael sat down to discuss the events with the rest of the group, and was soon up to date with everything that had gone on so far. But none of the others seemed to know anything about the assistance that might be arriving, and had never heard Peter and Julia speak of this woman before. Another coffee pot was brewed.

"Splendid!" Peter announced as he came back into the room. "She's available, and she'll be here before the week is out!"

CHAPTER ELEVEN

In the circumstances it was difficult for the group to know how to progress to the next step, although the state of Philip's eye was a reminder of how things had turned. To the obvious astonishment of the younger members Peter suggested they should simply stop. Bring in all the equipment and gather it in the dining room. Then perhaps they should stick to the front of the house and the kitchen. Of course this would include walking past the entrance to the tunnel every time they wanted a cup of tea or coffee but that was a minor inconvenience.

Even Peter had to admit, as excited as he was, he was starting to feel out of his depth. But there was method to his madness. Gathering the equipment together and setting about the task of checking and rearranging it gave everyone something to put their mind to and would keep them away from the rest of the house, giving them a little respite. Peter was conscious of the fact that the arrival of strangers can sometimes upset the spiritual world. In his mind, at least, perhaps everyone needed a break: spirits included. No argument came from anyone. Keeping in close quarters they collected all the apparatus, though no one mentioned collecting anything from the crypt.

Michael and Sarah were in one of the bedrooms, moving the sensors. They recognised one of the boxes that had been placed on a shelf. It was an old hamper that had lost its original purpose and become filled with any number of things that rarely got to see the light of day but were too important to be thrown away. It was too tempting for them not to miss a quick reminisce down memory lane. Inside they found pictures of their parents and a handful of holiday snaps. They momentarily lost track of time, scanning through and showing each other little details that the other may have missed.

"There's definitely something missing with the modern way of keeping photos, don't you think?" asked Michael.

"Yeah there's something nice about being able to touch them," his sister replied.

Just after she'd said this she let out a gasp and cupped her hand over her mouth before passing the photo she'd been looking at to Michael.

It was a family photo of all four of them having a picnic in the grounds. How they had never seen it before was astonishing: the housekeeper's face clearly visible in the kitchen window.

"My God! How did no one pick that up?" He shuddered as he put it in his pocket.

"What are you doing?"

"Keeping it for later; you know, for this person that's meant to be sorting things out."

"Not sure it's quite like that Michael," she said, questioning his optimism.

He just looked at her. It was weird not having Dad around and the photo brought him back to the forefront of his mind. The last few days had plastered over the cracks of their grief, but opening the box had only served to reopen that crack and that was maybe not such a good idea.

Sarah was having thoughts of her own but kept it to herself. Was their father now part of the fabric of the house, she wondered? Was he, too, trapped here like the others? Surely only bad spirits remained imprisoned like that? But then the playful giggles that they'd all heard suggested not.

Everyone gathered in the dining room, not just prepping the equipment but also to gather their thoughts. Peter was still visibly excited, even though he had calmed since their first arrival and the experiences they'd all been through. Time, however, was running out. The team had never meant to stay so long and they had their lives to get back to. Just as Michael did. And Sarah? Would she go back with Michael? Surely there was no way she could stay here on her own?

It felt odd to have a member missing. Only Julia herself felt that she wouldn't be missed. Her lack of confidence and self-worth often diminished how, in her mind, she thought other people saw her. Of course this was not the case and they all, especially Jane, wanted her back. It was also very unnerving that the very reason she wasn't there was the thing they feared now.

There were two more nights before the new team member arrived, and the team had made themselves comfortable at the front of the house. They went in pairs to the kitchen and never did leave anyone alone. The three younger members had contemplated sleeping in the van but even though things had become scary, staying outdoors was no sanctuary. Quietly Paul sat and wondered to himself if anyone would go with him should his stomach fail him in the night. He guessed he would find out but hoped he wouldn't need to.

On the first evening everything they needed was in the one room, and it had been reaffirmed that no ghost hunting would take place. They would sit it out until a new plan of action was decided upon.

"So!" Michael broke a mid-conversational silence, seizing his opportunity. "Who's this new person then, Peter?"

"Ah, yes, of course, Michael. She is a very old friend of mine." Peter leant into the group, motioning everyone to come closer, like a storyteller with a class of young children. "We went to university together, or rather we met there. We clicked straight away due to our interest in the paranormal. It wasn't until sometime later she confessed she could see people that had passed over – that's how she put it, back then. It's something that she keeps to herself, mainly because most don't believe in it."

As Peter paused footsteps could be heard in the room above them, but although they all looked up no one interrupted. They definitely would not be investigating this time. Peter gave an account of his friend's experiences and told them that it was a part-time thing that she kept to herself so as not to suffer ridicule. The only people she dealt with were those in need of her services.

"You see, the thing is, she only really deals with the very bad cases; she can communicate directly with them. It can be a little terrifying on occasions I can certainly attest," he concluded

It seemed to have been an unspoken group decision not to ask precisely what Peter could attest to. There was already enough for their minds to deal with in the here and now.

"So we're a really bad case then?" asked Sarah.

"Yes, or a good one, depending on your perspective." Peter smiled but his attempt at humour seemed to have drawn a blank with his audience.

The evening was spent chatting, in part to divert their thoughts but as much to just enjoy each other's company. Eventually their engagement trailed off and one by one they fell asleep. They were so tired that the small child that only now showed itself in full corporeal form did not wake them. It seemed to be in a playful mood as it moved between them, gazing up, as if lost in a sea of time. It danced between the members of the group. Jane murmured in her sleep as the spectre brushed past her, causing the blanket that was wrapped around her on the chair to slip from her lap. It carried on for a little while, as if lost in its own environment and only now discovering something new. It sat down in front of the fire and crossed its legs before disappearing again. The only real sound came from the clock in the hall that still kept its nightly vigil. Every light was out in the house and along with the grounds it lay in total darkness. An eerie silence descended and all was still.

Paul stirred; in need of the loo again. Long gone were the days when he could get through a set of nights without the need to pee and he was still only young, he thought to himself. As he begrudgingly brought himself to his senses, he looked around and saw everyone else was sound asleep. He too whished he was; especially under the circumstances. He was jittery and did not want to be the only one conscious but that's the way it was. As nervous as he was he wasn't about to upset anyone by waking them. He grabbed his phone, turned on the light, made for the door and skulked through to the hallway. His entire body was alight with trepidation. He didn't know how he would cope if he encountered anything on his own. There was absolutely no way he was about to go upstairs. He went as quickly as he could to the front door, not daring to look left or right, up or down.

These big flowerpots are bloody handy, he thought to himself. He had needed to go more than he realised. Once finished he now felt safer outside than he had done inside and took more notice of his peripheral vision, tentatively looking to his left and right. He almost lost his nerve when he saw a movement on the lawn but it was just the fox, sitting on the grass with one leg cocked behind its ear in a seemingly caressing motion. The two of them gave each other a few moments of their attention. The visiting creature gave him pause for thought. How is it that he – he assumed it was a he, but the sex of a fox is difficult to tell unless you're on slightly more friendly terms – could walk the grounds without a care and with no unwelcome attention being thrust upon it from the things that stalked this part of the countryside. The fox, apparently having better and more urgent affairs to attend to, put down its foot, craned its body and trotted off into the distance.

Paul, having now pondered on things that stalked the night, was on his own again and all too aware that he now had to cross the threshold between the hall and where the group were sleeping. What if, when he went back inside, there was something there in the darkness waiting specifically for his return? He took a moment to steady himself before bursting through the large front doors. As it turns out, that was as far as his nerves were going to hold out. He shut his eyes the rest of the way and just went where his nose pointed. He was safe! Thank God! As he settled back to sleep he wondered if he was ever going to get used to this ghost-hunting lark.

Nothing much else took place for the rest of that night or the one that followed. Apart from the giggles and footsteps, of course; it would have felt almost odd not to have those now. The inactivity in itself was unnerving. Sarah wondered if the things that haunted the house had heard their discussions and were waiting for the final fall of the curtain.

Michael was outside the front of the house savouring his coffee when a green Morris Minor came trundling up the drive. It somehow fitted his imaginings of the woman Peter had described. The stereotype he had in mind persisted until the door swung wide open, creaking as it did so. Out stepped a woman, younger looking than Michael was expecting. Her age didn't seem to match Peter's and his story that they went to university together. She wore a pleated skirt, smart brown shoes and a flowery top, with glasses that had tipped to the end of her nose as she got out of the car. Her hair was drawn back from her face into a chignon with whispery bits escaping the sides. Every inch an academic from Michael's perspective.

He almost choked on his slurp of coffee as she came hopping and skipping across to introduce herself; definitely Peter's friend he thought.

"Hello!" She used her forefinger to slide the bridge of her glasses up to the top of her nose. "Oh my, you poor things, you poor, poor things," she added before he could say a word.

Michael felt awkward and wasn't sure what to say or where exactly to position himself.

She continued unabated. "How long, how… ah, oh now this is something different."

Her head moved in stages as she took stock of the house, and she looked just about to follow her spiritual nose when she stopped and turned back to Michael.

"Sorry, how rude; I'm Andrea." She poked out a hand to shake Michael's.

It unsettled him, as he introduced himself, the length of time Andrea took holding his hand, a concerned expression on her face.

"Pleased to meet you," she finally said. "I'm assuming you know all about me." Before Michael could reply she was marching steadfastly to the large front doors.

"What a wonderful house!"

Peter heard her voice and at once leapt up. "Andrea!" he cried.

Andrea responded with what Michael was sure was a squeal of excitement.

"It's good to see you, old friend." Peter hugged her warmly, took her by the hand and led her in for introductions. They moved into the next room, taking their places around the table. All were eager to know more and just what this new visitor would bring.

Paul called Julia to let her know Andrea had arrived, and returned to say she would stay in the village for one more night to allow Andrea to gain a sense of the place. She would return in the morning.

The moment Andrea stepped inside there were faint footsteps in the room above. No one mentioned them, just glanced at each other with a nonchalant acceptance of what was now normality.

Andrea could sense that this was just the start. The sprits would want to let themselves be known to this new person, to, as Andrea was perhaps herself feeling, this intruder. For that reason she suggested they hold a séance that evening. The dining room table was cleared and Andrea placed a deep red taffeta cloth over it that she pulled from her large carpet bag before arranging two large candlesticks at either end along the centre line of the table. A third and larger one was set in the centre, and next to it a small tattered matchbox with the drawer open.

"I usually prefer more of a circle but this table will have to do. We'll sit on either side and the ones left at each end will make a connection by holding hands with the rest of us." She pinched a hair from the cloth with forefinger and thumb.

She asked Sarah for the largest mirrors in the house and to position one at each end of the table. They were old and had a patina of age, lending an instant eerie feel to the room. In between the comings and goings someone had sneaked in a coffee pot which was swiftly removed by Andrea, clearly somewhat narked by it being placed on the table at all.

At around seven thirty all was ready, and the séance was set for ten o'clock, as Andrea felt this to be a good time to call upon the entities and spirits that she was feeling were already constantly with her. Their presence, she told them, had been getting louder and louder since she arrived, some more so than others.

In the meantime they tucked into a meat stew cooked by Sarah earlier that day. When the time came, with echoes of a funeral march into a chapel, they filed behind one another into the dining room and took their places. Paul had shown due diligence and seen to his toiletry needs beforehand. Andrea was the last to sit.

On this night no equipment had been set up and the house lay, once again, in darkness. The room in which they now sat was slowly brought to light with each candle being lit by the strike of the matches before the box was placed back in its exact location. Michael noticed a certain sense of poetry to the ritual. Two small lamps were also used that gave a dull glow. Sarah took note of the candles and felt she knew why they were being used from what she'd learnt from Julia. She would keep an eye out for any movement of the flames this evening.

There was now complete silence in the room. Without any instruction they had all stopped talking. It was almost hypnotic. Almost relaxing. There was a certain therapeutic essence to the low light of a quiet room. The gentle illumination from the candles underlit the faces of all who now sat at the table. Holding hands they waited. Andrea told Peter to press record. She then asked who, in the spirit world, was now present with them. Who might step forward and communicate.

"I see a small boy," she announced to the group almost immediately. "I know you are here. Be brave, little one, come forward. We are here for you. That's it, come forward, tell me your name. You are safe here."

The rest of the group stayed nervously silent. Sarah thought she saw the reflection of something in one of the mirrors. Andrea was looking at something engaged in a conversation that the group was not part of. "You are a brave little one, thank you for coming to see us." She paused before continuing. "Ah, I see, that is good. And tell me how old are you? Ah! A big boy now."

She looked around the group. "He tells me he is seven. And learning his times tables. He's showing me how he uses his fingers to count. He is a lovely little chap. He is the one that moves things."

Andrea looked back down. "He's whispering to me now. He doesn't like the bad man. He's nasty, he tells me. He also says he stays away when he comes. He met him once and couldn't breathe, he was so afraid."

She raised her head again. "He's off playing now; he doesn't seem to know how long he has been here in this house. But I sense it has been a while… I'm not even certain he knows he is dead. He used to play with you two when you were both young. You were both blissfully unaware. Such a lovely little thing."

Sarah felt awful, so sad to hear of this little boy who had wanted to play with them yet they never knew he was there. Michael sat with his own unspoken thoughts. The room flickered from the candlelight. It seemed something else was now communicating with Andrea as the little boy dematerialised back into the shadows.

At that moment the door to the room opened with a slow, heavy groan. Nothing could be seen, just a cold presence felt, as if a wintery chill had crept in from an open front door. The candles flickered and died leaving only the dull glow of the lamps lighting the room. The floorboards creaked; something was moving across them.

Andrea remained focused. She was seeing a man. Mr Tolhurst! A rare appearance but tonight he had chosen to show himself once more. He moved with a stern authoritative motion towards the group, his eyes on Andrea with a look of firm contemplation. The boy was his son. Andrea could feel it. This man was condemned to wander the house without ever seeing him. Always knowing he was there but they were on different wavelengths. It was his cross to bear, the punishment for his actions in life. He had been a stern master when he had owned the land and built a lot of the structure of the house they were in now. A complex character who Andrea could sense was full of hate, love and regret. He was alone, even though the mother of the child was haunting the grounds too. He continued through the room before disappearing though the wall at the far end. Only Andrea could see him.

For a moment all was still. At Andrea's signal Peter lit the candles that had gone out.

"Now," she said, "we must wait a little longer. There are others here but it is unclear if they want to communicate. These are in more control of themselves. But something is definitely choosing not to come forward, a dark entity that menaces this house."

The long silence that followed was broken by a loud bang. It made everyone jump. From the hall they heard the screeching sound of a chair being launched across the floor. It hit the front internal doors so hard that the glass shattered and the wood splintered. Everyone but Andrea rushed out, forgetting the instruction not to break the circle. It was unnerving to see that the chair had again apparently moved of its own accord. But they knew something had forced it across the floor. The question they were asking themselves was what had pushed it and why the sheer violence behind the act? Peter examined the doors. Standing in the dark hall each of them felt it. A disturbance in the atmosphere that was greater, different from anything that had been experienced before. It was cold yet burning. They looked at one another to see if anyone could guess what it might be before turning to the obvious direction the presence was coming from. Before them was the answer.

It was the housekeeper.

CHAPTER TWELVE

It seemed like an age, but it was the housekeeper who was first to move. Her face was more human this time but her eyes were still vacant, as if missing but still there somehow. From where she still sat, Andrea could sense a real rage within this woman. A great deal of hurt. She moved slowly at first then with a howling scream she was upon them before any of them realised. Jane jumped backwards and found herself up against the wall. The spectre grew in size and seemed to envelop them. They could smell the fabric of her clothing, almost suffocating them. There was a groan, a deep disturbing groan. As the presence intensified Michael found the courage to shout, "What do you want?! Well!? Bloody well tell us!"

It was more an attempt to assuage his growing anxiety, but as to deny him the satisfaction of an answer the spectre simply vanished.

"Blimey, old chap," said Peter. "That was a bit out the blue, that one." Michael sensed that this was Peter's way to calm his own nerves.

"She's the boy's mother." Andrea was standing in the doorway. All this while she had been consumed by the thoughts and feelings that she sensed as she looked on at the haunting apparition, one that had found safety in the shadows with just the haunting eyes staring back in a fixed gaze. This once-living woman was now evidently trapped, forever searching, forever demanding what belonged to her.

"She fell in love with Mr Tolhurst."

They returned to the table, where Andrea explained that the boy that had been seen and heard was the inevitable result of the fruits of their love. But it came from the darkest depths of control and abuse. The master's will over his servant. It didn't make the man evil; it just made him what he was. A fragile insecure being with deep resentment for his own existence. Something that ate away at him, from a time when such things were not spoken of, a confusing mess of emotional turmoil. In his own way he loved her but could only show it in the way he knew how. Love and intimacy were scary to him. Such unresolved trauma had ultimately twisted his intentions and deformed any romantic intimacy with his lover. He had deeply respected her, indeed that was the attraction in the first place, but once she had given herself to him that respect was lost. Men often find connection though the physical act of love, but to him it was confusing, as if he had allowed himself to be vulnerable in a way that was an affront to him. The relationship was hidden but the housekeeper grew ever more dependent on his affections.

It was on their last night of passion that the boy was conceived, in the master's bedroom. When the pregnancy could no longer be hidden she was sent away for fear of a ruined reputation. But all along the mistress of the house knew. As women do. She knew her husband. The keeper was sent under the guise of duties to be taken elsewhere within the family's financial empire and holdings. She returned once the boy had been born. In the interim the mistress had been taken ill, her kindness been rewarded with death, and she had departed this world one night, succumbing to a terrible fever. It was her figure that had been seen in the grounds. The boy was to be brought up not knowing who his mother was. A ward of his father.

It was remarkable that none of the other servants ever knew of or indeed found out about the fruits of the affair, and it seemed that the story made sense to all who surrounded the boy. The housekeeper continued with her duties, always at arm's length from her child. Never was she to be allowed to be recognised in the child's affections other than as a servant. The pain grew, adding to a darkness that had already been sown. The child never grew to know his place in this world and one fateful day he was killed. So quick was the child's death and still so innocent was he that he still did not fully understand what had happened. He should have passed into the next life but he became trapped by the means of his death.

It was late one evening when it happened and the young boy was being affectionally watched from a distance by his mother. Being not allowed anywhere near her boy she could not protect him when the time came. She could only watch in horror from the upstairs window. Shouting as she attempted to alert him. The panic and horror would forever remain imprinted on her featureless ghostly expression.

The impact must have taken him quickly. A carriage racing towards the house. Instructed to do so by the master, who was late for one of his engagements. The child did not see the carriage wheel that crushed him. The next thing he knew he was playing with his toys again. The other world is a mysterious layer to the world we know. The veil that sometimes lifts is a mysterious winding path way that distorts memories and places a person out of sync with their once earthly bonds. It is why sometimes people stay and sometimes people visit. And why only sometimes an imprint of that memory stays. Apparitions can be a fickle thing.

The shock of the boy's death sent the mother to her own and she died there in the front of the house with the child' crumpled remains in her arms. Such was the sadness and rage of not being allowed to be with him that she blamed herself and condemned her soul to regret. So great was the hurt that it caused her to be much more than a spectre joining the ranks of the others in the house. Instead she became an entity with such self-awareness she could move objects and make her presence felt and seen when she wanted to. She was consumed with anguish in life and now with hatred in death. She stalked the halls looking for her boy; even in death the curse of not being allowed a motherly connection continued. Such was the veil which prevented the paths of the three from crossing. And the visitation of the master's wife? That kind soul. Andrea did not know if she would make her presence known again. She was there only to see the boy was protected. It was becoming clear to Andrea from who. But it would not be from the mother's curse.

In the light of this new information it was decided to start the séance again, with a mixture of trepidation and curiosity. How would this night continue? What new ghostly spectre might appear before the night gave over its grip to the day. The candles were relit and they held hands once more. The room was again held in the glow of the lamps and the burning candles. Andrea closed her eyes. Almost immediately footsteps began stalking the floor above them. Apart from Andrea, who kept her eyes closed, the group could not help but trace their route across the ceiling before they heard the sound of a door opening. The footsteps continued, then the creak of stairs being descended. Someone or something was coming to see them, it seemed. They gripped each other's hands tightly in an expectation of the heavy groan of the door. The footsteps could now be heard on the hard floor of the hall but they sounded as though they were going away from them... heading to the front room, whose door was heard opening then slamming shut. The loud bang made them jump again. Whatever it was, it was now in the front room, perhaps even wating for them there.

Andrea opened her eyes. "We must not be goaded. This new entity wants to break the circle, but our curiosity must not get the better of us."

Sarah noticed that not one candle flame flickered. She wasn't sure if this concerned her or not, but she saw that Michael had noticed it too.

CHAPTER THIRTEEN

A kind of haunting peacefulness brought its own sanctuary in the morning. All that had taken place the night before was being mentally absorbed. Michael's mental state, however, was starting to fracture. He could feel it, but for the time being the effects were only subtle and so could easily be pushed to the back of his mind. He could subdue it, at least for now.

Sarah woke that morning deep in thought and feeling somewhat melancholy; she really wanted to be left alone and to send everyone away. Everyone but Michael, of course. She wanted to have her dad back, and those first few days when Michael had arrived. The house felt too busy now and on this morning it was making her head hurt.

Peter was alone with Andrea, discussing what they should do next. "Is this a ghost hunt or are we turning into exorcists?" he asked.

"You don't have to say it with such a twinkle in your eye; it wouldn't mean a promotion, you know."

Philip, Paul and Jane were in the back of the van repairing some of the bulging boxes of equipment.

"So, last night then?" Paul began. That was a bit—"

He was interrupted by Philip. "Don't start, mate; this is far more than any of us thought we were getting into."

"This place is cursed alright. I'd rather not spend another night here to be honest," added Jane.

It was Jane who phoned Julia, summarised the night's events and arranged for Michael to pick her up around midday. Julia sat in her chair pondering. There was something that wasn't right about the whole situation but she couldn't put her finger on it. It just felt odd.

The day began like a military operation, the team determined to set everything up correctly and capture what they have been witnessing. The plan was to set up secret night cameras, in an attempt to fool the spirits, if such a thing could be done. First, Michael escorted Andrea around the entire house, so she could spend time in every room. Just standing there in silent contemplation. He felt a little awkward, like a spare part at a wedding, each time she closed her eyes and just stood there. Not saying a word. It was a slow process. Michael amused himself with his thoughts; it was a bit like taking Flint for a walk, and waiting every time for him to sniff around searching for the right moment to relieve himself. Thank God she doesn't need a shit, he thought.

While Michael was in this state of self-amusement Andrea was locked in her own thoughts, sensing and communicating with whatever it was walked the corridors. Rather like a general on the eve of battle she was preparing herself for the night ahead. She would open each door slowly, as if wanting to make herself known quietly before interrupting someone. Michael had come to the realisation that each time she did this she really was expecting someone to be in side, assuming she would be intruding on someone's privacy. This unsettled him a little: to think that you didn't have to wait for an entity to be known, that in fact they were already with you, that you were the intruder! Andrea didn't convey anything back to Michael, to have him as a guide was all she needed.

Meanwhile Sarah found that she was once again part of the team, as if she was there as a ghost hunter, not the owner. She didn't really mind as it seemed to help her mood. Phones and tablets had been put on charge and some were now showing green lights. Over every doorway they'd set up a thin wire and secured the bells from it once more. No doorway was left out. Every single room had at least two sensors and all the spares were used, giving some rooms three or even four. Sarah amused herself: Christ, she thought, someone's going to have a fit if this lot all goes off. The EVP readers too were placed in as many rooms as possible, although the team had fewer of them so there weren't enough for every location. Night cameras were set up in areas where visitations had been seen and a couple of wildlife cameras had been tied to a drainpipe and a tree in the hope of catching sight of the master's wife. Or indeed anything else that might want to let itself be captured.

So much had been going on that morning that it was a surprise to Michael that it was already past eleven. "Crikey, I'm meant to collect Julia. Andrea, I'll ask Sarah to take over from me."

He felt a little awkward just leaving her there but figured she'd be okay for a brief moment; besides, she looked like she knew what she was doing.

Sarah gave him an unexpected hug before she went upstairs to find Andrea. Michael clambered into the Defender and set off. The snow had almost completely retreated now and only a few stubborn clumps of ice lingered, collecting dirt and leaves. The fields were dotted with boulder-like ice sculptures. It didn't look like it would snow again.

The village was quiet when he pulled into the car park. As he walked to the B&B he felt frustrated that his mind was so clouded. The last few days had been harder to get through. He knew the sudden outburst in the hall wasn't just his nerves breaking or fright taking hold. It was depression gently rapping on his mental door. Intrusive thoughts, never too far away, another warning sign he would have been waiting for. He just wished he could shift and get rid of what he'd come to know as his stress head or depression headache.

There was no one to greet him when he walked through the door, so he waited out of politeness to the proprietor, to see if anyone would attend to him. After a few minutes, having never had much patience and a tendency to become irritable and intolerant of people's lack of urgency, especially at the moment, he decided to go and find Julia.

He found her in the conservatory, with a freshly brewed teapot evident from the steam coming out of its spout.

"Mind if I pour myself a cuppa?" he asked.

The sudden break in her reverie made her jump and made Michael chuckle.

"Oh, hello Michael, of course, yes there's plenty; it's just arrived actually, perfect timing." She held one hand on her chest to still her jolted heart.

They talked on the way back, much more than they had when they drove to the B&B. Julia seemed more together, and though Michael didn't really know why, this made him glad. Phillip was at the back of the van when they pulled into the drive.

"Julia!" Philip greeted her. "Good to have you back." He reached round with his spare hand to give a half-box-holding hug when she got out of the Land Rover.

"Hello, Philip. I hear you've all had an eventful time while I've been away."

"Yeah, just a bit, mate. We're setting the place up now. I tell ya, if it was explosives we'd be on the moon tonight." Philp rather wished he would be on the moon later.

"Julia!" Peter was his usual excitable self. "Andrea's somewhere abouts doing her stuff."

Andrea and Sarah had been joined by Jane as they swept the last few rooms, so it wasn't until they were back from the attic bedrooms that they knew Julia and Michael had returned. It was a late lunch that they all sat down to. Through the day everything had run like clockwork. There was a new and revitalised determination to learn more of this phenomenon and if possible to resolve it.

Michael nipped out to the 'shed' and was tinkering at the workbench when he heard a sound that he thought could only come from the house. The unmistakable sound of giggling. Here in the workshop, with him. Over in the corner was a staircase that led up to a mezzanine floor, where bits and pieces were stored such as old car parts, tools, lengths of wood, the odd painting and a mirror wrapped in hessian cloth. It was covered in dust and he wondered when anyone last went up those stairs. Michael's gaze instinctively directed him where his primal emotion thought he should look. To his amazement he could clearly see a pair of eyes staring down at him, though the face was obscured by the stair rail and accumulated junk.

Michael stood with his back to the worktop, keeping quite still and watching as the eyes flickered and moved. They were clearly keeping watch on him too. For a moment they disappeared and then just as suddenly reappeared again, this time within the clear corporeal form of the young boy. It seemed he had come to say hello. Michael's skin tingled with electricity, an uncontrollable response to seeing a child that he knew to be dead. Sadder somehow, than even the spectral housekeeper or anything else that had appeared, or might yet do so. The young boy merely giggled and skipped away into the yard before gently disappearing from sight.

Michael could not have explained why he decided not to say anything when he returned to the house. It was almost as if the boy had chosen him and was asking him to keep a secret. Michael felt honour bound to do so, like an uncle promising not to get his nephew in trouble with his parents over some misdemeanour.

It was now very late afternoon and the feeling of foreboding had grown once again. It had begun its constriction upon the house and all those within, as they anticipated the night ahead, like a hand tightening around the throat. Sarah sat by the fire, her anxiety returning. She had felt on edge for most of the day. Paul was checking one of the laptops. The others had gathered in the dining room preparing for the séance, apart from Michael, who was in the kitchen making a pot of coffee. His mind was wired and he couldn't switch it off. Lots of things were on his mind but he kept returning to one in particular. The crypt. It was such a weird thing to have in your garden, and while he knew it would have been there long before the house was built it was a strange occurrence to end up with such a thing nonetheless. He got out his phone and scrolled though pictures of Flint. There was even one which had his sister Dyna in, a snapshot of her in the garden taking ownership of a stolen tub of butter. The pictures helped calm his mind a little.

He was still thinking of the history of the house, why there were so many entities associated with it and why they should all make themselves known now. Same questions, still no answer he thought. The house was growing cold. The kind of coldness that enters your body and stays in your bones. People donned an extra layer and all of the downstairs fires were lit. Still the coldness persisted. It coursed through every part of the house and settled like ice in their veins.

It was time for the séance to get underway. Peter and Andrea thought it would be beneficial to hold it in the hall this time. It seemed to them to make sense; a focal point, an exact middle ground and where a lot of the encounters were starting to happen. It was not lost on Michael that the location was closer to the entrance leading to the crypt. The table was set once again, only this time the smaller one from the kitchen. This circle would be very intimate in this séance. Peter sat at the end with his back to the front door and Andrea to his side. Holding hands around this table involved resting their forearms flat on the surface. They placed themselves below the great chandelier; Philip looked a little worried about this but chose not to voice his opinions. Candles were lit; two large white ones on the table and smaller ones in a circle around them on the floor.

Michael looked at the arrangement and could see the team were going all out on this one. The house lights were turned off. The candles were all that remained. Everyone was given a pocket torch, in case things got a little disturbing and they were separated. Such had become the expectation of what the house could offer.

The coldness crept around them and the candles flickered. Certainly something was making itself known. The veil between the two worlds was beginning to weaken again. Paul noticed a slight movement in the chandelier; looking at Jane he could see that she'd seen it too. The clock chimed; eight o'clock. All was very still. Then a sound, very faint, could be heard coming from the top of the house. If it was audible in the hall, Michael thought, the source must be quite loud given its source. It sounded like a rocking chair being rocked back and forth. It stopped. Then began again, faster in rhythm than before. Faster and faster until the sound abruptly stopped once more. Followed by a knocking, a slow rhythmic knocking, but that wasn't what it was. Michael realised it was coming down the stairs; something had been set in motion, carrying itself knocking or rather thumping down each step. They kept quite still as the candles continued to flicker without the slightest movement of air. The thumping stopped and now the sound of a ball rolling across the first landing was heard before it thudded against the skirting.

Andrea cleared her throat, more as an indication to the others she was about to speak than out of necessity. "Who are you?" she asked in a soft, empathetic tone. "Speak to us now, be known to us, who are you?" she repeated.

Only Andrea and Peter could see what was approaching. At first it looked like the figure of the housekeeper emerging from the shadowy darkness of the hall but Andrea quicky realised it was something else, something darker than its surroundings and indeed something darker by nature. Something that had travelled to the house from the crypt.

Two loud echoing thumps were heard as if in response to the questions, nothing more.

Then silence.

An eerie stillness was present. Then a pair of eyes like polished jet shone back through the night.

"Tell us again, please let yourself be known to us."

The walls shook. It was as if a giant had picked up a snow globe that the house lay in, and to Philip's alarm the light above them swung violently as the bells across the door frames began to shake. Behind Peter the two damaged delicate internal doors were pulled open. Then another loud thump, louder than anything that had come before, sending a crack running along the wall from the top of the stairs. Yet the circle remained resolute. A latent groan could be heard; gradually developing into a deep visceral growl. Slowly it melted into the background.

Now the stillness returned but with no offer of relief. It was heavy with nefarious intent.

CHAPTER FOURTEEN

The hall remained icy cold. The internal doors rattled. The groan returned. It seemed to be coming from the depths of the house. Where exactly, this time no one could determine. But still it continued to come. It was a terrible, painful groan, getting louder and louder before it abruptly stopped.

"Who is it? Who is there? We know you are not with us but you are here somewhere in this house aren't you?" Andrea was reaching out.

The sound of the rocking chair returned, with a methodical knocking. It became a constant sound in the background. It was loud yet seemed to be in a far distant space echoing thorough time. If it was intended to discomfit the group it was working. Then, it stopped again, and at first no one noticed this had coincided with the appearance of the housekeeper standing to the side of Peter in the doorway. They gasped as they saw it; they had become accustomed to this spectre but she still struck a primeval fear into them every time she showed herself.

"Please, don't stay out of the circle, come to us," Andrea called out, and Michael wondered if she was talking to the housekeeper or to something else that had appeared out of his eyeline.

The candles lapped the cold air as the figure moved towards them. It was a surreal moment when this thing from the world beyond sat upon an unoccupied chair, quite confidently, beside them.

"Thank you," Andrea acknowledged her.

Philip and Paul were clearly none too happy and Jane looked like she was about to pass out. Julia just looked at the figure, compelled but with a disturbed expression. Peter was obviously captivated. Michael and Sarah both fixed their gaze on this visitor of their home. The bony fingers stretched out and rested on the table as the candles flames withered and barely kept alight.

From outside, the house would have looked quite normal to anyone passing in the night. Had they looked more closely however, and should they be open to such sights, they would have seen the ghostly apparition of the master's wife, gliding just a little above the grassy ground as if looking in vain for a way in. What the passer-by could not have known was the torment this apparition was enduring. She could sense the night unfolding and was desperate to find the boy, but every time she came close to the house she would disappear, only to quickly reappear and repeat the process. She had become stuck, yet she sensed that this night was to be different. As if she knew what was coming. She was half attached to this world and half to the next, conscious but with muddled thought, unsure of her role other than to repeat her desire to protect.

Inside, the housekeeper remained quite still as the door to the tunnel began creaking on its hinges. Through the wall walked the figure of the master of the house. Immediately the housekeeper let out a terrifying scream and rose from her seat before launching it over Peter's head to crash into the front doors. The figure of Mr Tolhurst seemed to fluctuate between a corporeal form and an unbodied one as the chandelier hanging above them suddenly flashed into a brilliant white light. When Michael opened his eyes the two entities were gone but the entrance to the tunnel was clear. The boarding had been ripped aside and the door barely clung to its hinges. Darkness fell once again; only the outer candles offered light, oddly remaining lit.

Everyone was looking at Andrea. Wanting to know what to do next.

"Well, that was all very interesting, wasn't it," she said calmly. "I think that maybe we should pair off in teams of two now. I sense they are spreading themselves out."

"Bit risky isn't it?" Peter interjected, leaning in to whisper in her ear.

Andrea smiled. "Perhaps, but we must analyse and adapt, and move with what they are trying to convey to me on this night."

And so they paired up. Michael with Sarah, of course, Andrea and Jane, Philip and Julia, and Peter and Paul (hope we don't become two little dickie birds, thought Paul to himself). They left the candles where they were and set off with their torches. Michael reflected that the torches were meant to be for emergency use in case they were separated, and now here they were deliberately doing exactly that. But it clearly made sense to Andrea and the group had put their faith in her.

They abandoned the lower floor, agreeing if the crypt were, as seemed inevitable, to play a part in the night's proceedings then they could return. Tentatively they ascended the stairs splitting into their separate routes on the first landing. Philip went ahead of Julia; twisting the end of the torch to focus the light on the first corridor. They didn't give a great deal of illumination but then that was the point. Part of the night's investigation was to remain in the dark, keep in the shadows and not to disturb the environment they were in or risk uninviting those they wanted to invite. Slowly and quietly they went, disappearing into the gloom.

Peter and Paul took the second corridor that led off to the right, torchlight darting across the walls and beyond until they too disappeared. On the next floor Andrea and Jane went into the first of the grand bedrooms, Jane keeping close to Andrea's side. Finally Michael and Sarah climbed slowly to the very top and entered the servants' corridor.

Philip and Julia had ventured into one of the first-floor bedrooms. "Can you sense anything?" Philip asked, turning his head to Julia.

"No, nothing yet."

This particular bedroom hadn't been used in years. There was an old bare-framed Victorian bed, a low-backed chair and a toy chest against one wall. The mantelpiece had a layer of dust coating its surface. Philip shivered as he noticed the dainty prints of a child's fingers. It was evident someone or something hadn't abandoned the room entirely. He backed away and bumped into Julia before showing her the prints, but Julia couldn't pick up any emotions that were attached to them.

She looked at Philip. "There's someone new here."

As Julia uttered these words Philip became aware of something in the corner, moving in the shadows, its eyes looking back at them. Its small stature suggested this was the owner of the prints. Philip slowly moved the beam of his torch from the floor to the corner, and was startled to see it scurry to avoid the light. At that moment the door to the bedroom slammed shut! Philip struggled with the handle and pulled at it as the thing crawled from the shadows. Getting closer, Julia felt its presence touch her soul. If Philip had been able to see he would have noticed that Julia suddenly looked ever so pale. But his attention was all on how to get out.

Their struggle and his shouts for help were not heard by the others. Somehow, it seemed, in that room their voices were held in a field of silence. Without knowing it they had been placed in an entirely different time from the one when they had entered.

At the very top of the house Michael and Sarah remained unaware of anything that was occurring. Each doorway cast its unique personality outwards into the unnervingly silent, dark corridor. Every floorboard they stepped on creaked, only adding to the eeriness that was playing on their nerves. They walked the length of the corridor to its end. It took courage to walk past each blank void that was an open door. They turned and looked back into the passageway of darkness. The old yellowing paint of the door frames, architrave and skirting gave out an uncared-for feeling that shone faintly in the darkness. The doorknobs were loose in their housings and would easily rattle but nothing moved. It was so silent. They looked at each other; should it really be this quiet? Michael turned up the beam of his torch and shone it back along the corridor.

"OH MY GOD!" yelled Sarah.

"What in God's name is that!" said Michael, his voice breaking into a tremor.

Before them, though they did not know it, was the very thing that had been on this spot since time itself had shaped the land. It grew out of the darkness of the corridor and stood before them in all its malevolent evil. Showing itself in their presence, in its full form for the very first time.

It touched the floor with the tips of its clawed wraith toes; there was a bodily form to this being while at the same time it had no body at all. Even the darkness retreated from it, leaving a grotesque hollow around its form. The feet were grey and stained with blood. The nails were black. Above them hung a tattered cloth resembling an ancient, worn-out cloak which hung awkwardly on the hunkered frame. The arms were outstretched to the side, the hands almost scraping the walls. Its head was cast down between its shoulders, moving slowly like the pendulum of a clock. Its form somehow took over the space within the corridor entirely and completely.

Knowing nothing could be done, they stood with their backs to the wall looking at what was approaching them with what seemed a cruelly deliberate slowness. This other thing from another world, another realm. From a place neither wanted to visit or even know. Both of them wanted to find a way to speak, to ask the other what it was. But their mouths were dry and the fear of speech created its own silence. As their nerves began to spike in response to the situation, the whole house shook, with such violence that cracks raced across the walls. The old lath and plaster capitulated to the tremors and the corridor filled with dust as the shaking became so strong that even some of the slats gave way and splintered like broken limbs.

Cloaked in darkness, the thing raised its head to look at them with unmistakable contempt and suspicion. There were no eyes, no structure to the face, but a face nonetheless. Like a wolf eyeing its prey, deciding when and how to strike, the head tilted from one side to the other.

From the focus of such forces the house was in danger as much as its occupants were. On this plot of land it had by accident rather than any malevolent design acted as a conduit, a perfect gateway between two worlds that was, for the most part, kept shut and acted much like a cell, containing those that came and could not leave. All these past days were now accumulating to an ending.

Sarah could not understand why her screams were not being heard or even at least in some way affecting the apparition. Not even the shaking of the house had brought anyone running to investigate. Only now did she realise her screams were silent. No sound was coming out of her mouth. The figure stood still with a clear meaning behind its gaunt face; a warning to leave! As if in recognition of her understanding, it began to fade and melt away into the darkness, yet it could still be seen watching. They saw their chance and made a dash down the corridor. Their bodies felt hollow and the adrenaline was still coursing through their veins when they ran straight into Andrea and Jane in the middle of the lower corridor. Andrea instantly took in the look on their faces.

"Did you two or any other fucker not hear that!" Michael shouted, his anger born partly out of the fear that was still filtering his emotions and partly out of frustration that they should have been left alone by the investigating team to cope with what they had just faced.

Andrea stepped forward, almost brushing Jane to the side in her focus on Michael and Sarah, sensing the energy that they had encountered. It was still with them, in a manner of speaking. Such was the power of the entity.

"What exactly did you just encounter?" she asked.

Sarah stepped forward, as angry and shaken as her brother. "You mean you two heard nothing of what just happened. The whole bloody house was shaking for Christ sake! Go and see for yourself! The walls almost split in two."

Michael put his hand out. "No way; no one's going back up there right now."

"We must, I must!" Andrea protested.

"If you'd just seen what we have, you wouldn't want to," Michael stressed. "There's something hideous here and I'll be dammed if it's going to drive us away, but right now my arsehole is going ten to the dozen. Where is everyone else anyway?"

There was a sternness in his features that was new to Andrea, and as the other three set off to find her colleagues she deliberately hung back. When she felt sure no one was looking she left and made her way to the top corridor. She was scared, true enough, but she could not resist following her instincts. For there was something that she had never told anyone about how she had become the way she was.

CHAPTER FIFTEEN

Andrea was special. She had always been told she was. When she was very young she could sense things others could not. But there was more to her than this. Once, when she was in her first flush of youth and venturing on her first holiday without parental guidance, she had ventured into a little village. A row of cottages next to an old church with a graveyard populated with headstones in a well-mannered intimacy. It was raining hard. She had arrived on the back of a motorbike with new friends she had made on her journey. They decided to take refuge under the lychgate of the church from the growing intensity of the rain that was surely threatening a storm. She ignored her instincts about the place and followed their group leader into the unlocked church for better shelter. It was dark, and two large candles flickered as they opened the door. Andrea noticed something dashing by her out of the rain.

The headstones all seemed very new, and the last date on the largest one by the door read 1752. As they sat down with no one else around, she mused on this; it wasn't the date specifically, it was that it could be read with such astonishing clarity. That shouldn't be, should it? And the stones? Most stood clean and upright, barely one tilting or showing little sign of lichen. She could hear the downpour of the rain. It thundered on the roof and a crack of lighting shot across the sky and lit up the stained glass giving a prism of beautiful light through the church. It didn't concern Andrea or her companions and they felt safe in their shelter. They got comfortable for the night ahead.

Something was strange, in the morning, when they left; there was not a car in sight on any of the lanes. Come to think of it, they hadn't seen anyone since yesterday. Looking back at the church it seemed the storm had taken a greater toll on its Norman tower than they had realised with sections of the merlons dislodged and fallen to the ground. All the more strange that no one should be about. They rode only a short distance that day and camped not far away. Andrea's instincts were playing on her and so she decided to make her way back to the village. This time there were cars parked in the lane, but where the row of cottages had been there were modern houses and as for the church, the church had all but gone. All that was left was the narthex through which they'd entered, but now barely visible through the undergrowth.

At this age Andrea was new to such weird experiences and couldn't understand what had just happened. Instead she convinced herself she had gone the wrong way and this was a different village; English villages all look much alike. Turning to leave, still somewhat unnerved by her experience, she saw a hooded figure walking near where she knew the headstones should be. This figure seemed not to have noticed her when to her amazement it began to rise higher, as if climbing a stairwell that no longer existed. Now Andrea remembered the stairs inside the church and realised she was in the same village where they'd stayed the night before.

The spectre disappeared and Andrea decided it was time to go back to her friends. But her visions would never leave after that day and her connection with what she would come to know as the spirit world became like a second home to her, only becoming stronger as the years passed. That visit to that village from a time out of sync with her own merely enhanced her natural abilities and changed her forever.

All alone now, she entered the top of the narrow stairs that twisted into the corridor where Michael and Sarah had their encounter. The darkness was interjected with a grey mist that seemed to orbit through the air. She knew she wasn't alone through her connection with the other world. She was also aware that whatever it really was that was with her now knew she was there and was waiting for her to make the first move. Her breath broke through the mist; it was so cold. She stood where Michael and Sarah had been and faced the wall. She could feel the presence behind her.

"Hang on, where's Andrea?" asked Peter, as Michael looked around to take stock of who was among the group that had assembled in the hallway. Philip and Julia were missing too. Before anyone could stop him Peter made a dash for the stairs, calling her name. Michael led the way to the first floor, flinging open the closed bedroom door. Inside, the moment it opened time seemed to shudder and Philip and Julia came to their senses, bewildered and wondering just what had just happened.

"You two okay?" asked Paul.

"I don't know, exactly." Philip looked at Julia as if for an explanation.

Julia looked around the room before saying simply, "Yes, but let's get out of here though."

"I can't find her." Peter appeared behind them, his usual stoic composure gone and looking quite panic stricken. "She's just not here!" He looked puzzled and bereft of answers.

"She hasn't come this way," said Paul.

"Bloody hell, I told her to stay with us." Michael was obviously just as irritated by the fact that now he'd have to go and find her.

Staying together this time, they searched every level and every room, until as a last resort they made their way to the crypt, to find her lying unconscious against the wall.

"Andrea! Wake up! Andrea!!" Peter demanded.

They couldn't use phones in the crypt to call for help and decided to take her back to the house. That wouldn't be possible using the tunnel, so they'd have to take her up the stairs, along the sloping passageway and into the grounds. It was decided the group should split up so they could go in both directions. After all they all had the same destination. Michael picked Andrea up in his arms; she was still unresponsive.

"You go first," said Michael to Peter. "We can only go up one at a time." While the two of them made their way up the steps the others headed back to the house through the tunnel. Entering the hall they found furniture had been thrown around and the lights had blown. There was broken glass and smashed wood everywhere. The chandelier lay in pieces on the floor.

He didn't much like being the last to leave but there wasn't much else he could do. At the top of the slope Peter tuned to give Michael a hand and to support Andrea, desperate now to get her back to the house in the hope that the others had got there already and phoned for an ambulance.

A short distance away there was something watching. In fact it was someone, with a tear gently rolling down their cheek. Andrea could see them carrying her body from the crypt. She understood at once what the crypt was for. Her body had now replaced that of the ancient figure that haunted the land, that had been imprisoned, walled up thousands of years ago in a tomb that lay beneath the crypt. And when this was built over, it had carried the curse. She understood completely and every little detail was clear to her now. She had been taken in that corridor. In a way she had always been meant to be taken in that corridor, ever since the day she was born. She was always meant to have come to this place. People like her are rare and when they enter this world these beings know, they feel their time may come. All that had happened up to this point now seemed preordained.

The walk back to the house with Andrea in Michael's arms was a surreal moment. Peter shone his torch to lead the way. Entering the hall they saw the others waiting.

"Ambulance?" Michael asked.

Philip waved his phone in the air. "Nothing, we've got nothing. The phones are dead and there's no landline."

Michael took Andrea into the dining room and placed her on the table, all too aware of the chaos and destruction around them.

"Lights?" Peter asked, trying the switch.

"Nothing mate, bulbs are all smashed," answered Paul.

"How is she?" Sarah asked, the first to do so in all the hurry and confusion.

Michael checked her pulse. "Still with us, but barely; Christ's sake how the hell did she get into the crypt and why? No one saw her leave, did they?" He looked around the room for answers. Only blank faces and shakes of the head answered.

"Andrea! Come on, girl, come back to us, come on!" But Michael's request went unanswered. She lay on the table, face ashen, unmoving.

"Fuck, fuck me!" Paul's outburst broke the solemn atmosphere and everyone looked to see what it was.

Outside, looking in through the window was the housekeeper. This time, however, there was a sense of understanding in her face, a display of empathy from this previously bitter and careworn creature. Pity for Andrea, Sarah thought. She slowly pivoted and moved away.

"I've had just about enough of this bullshit," Michael declared.

Peter scrambled through his pockets for his car keys. "I'll take her to the village, get help there."

Michael carried Andrea out and gently rested her in the passenger seat. "Right, you okay then Peter? If you still can't get a signal go straight to the B&B; they'll be the most likely to answer at this time of night I should think."

"Yes, good show." Peter started the engine and wiggled the gear lever. But it wasn't to be that easy. A dark entity blocked the car's exit. Peter swerved and crashed into a gatepost as the others ran to the car.

Paul got to the driver's door first. Peter had hit his head on the steering wheel and his response was somewhat groggy but he said he was okay. Andrea was carefully laid back on the table with a blanket for warmth. All of a sudden they were at a loss as what to do.

Andrea may still have been with them in physical form but her time in the living world was fast coming to an end. She had been caught in the net of the afterlife. The entity that had played the long game so well and consumed her had been created in a time lost to history. Once it had been a living person, who was used and tortured by the community they lived in. They became twisted, filled with hate and evil intent until, when finally they had been used as much as anyone could be, they were walled up and forgotten about. The spirit of this dead person bound in fetters continued its insidious progress and filled the land with its dark seed. Anyone who knew would have been wise enough to leave the land alone and never to disturb it.

Sid was right: the land was much older than the house. A monastery once stood on the site and slowly passed into ruin before eventually disappearing from living memory. Only the crypt above the tomb lay forgotten, abandoned, left behind. It had been too many centuries now for the spirit to be saved in any meaningful way, no séance could help this being. It was evil and its hold on the land is what had trapped the other spirits when they became stuck between the two worlds.

"Stuff this, we've got to do something." Michael looked at Sarah, and not for approval.

Sarah had seen her brother in this mood before. Whatever it was he decided there would be very little anyone could do to stop him.

He pointed at Peter. "Get Andrea out of here.

Sarah caught up with him as he stormed out of the house.

"What are you up to?

"Take someone with you and get anything you need or want to take," he replied curtly.

Heading for the shed, Michael set about his task like a member of special forces. Inside the shed he gathered up empty jars, jerrycans, old oil drums. He emptied the petrol out of the lawnmower and soaked some rags in it. He got more from siphoning his car. He stacked all of this outside, just in time to see the fox scurry off. Sarah thought she knew what was happening but couldn't quite believe it.

The team members were now frantically gathering up their equipment, thinking they were being driven out by a madman, but they'd had enough and were happy to be leaving. What the hell was this situation anyway? It had started off as part of their hobby, just another investigation with a few ringing bells, but had become this nightmarish hell. As they went from one area to the next, unknown to them they were followed by the little boy.

Sarah hurried to their father's bedroom and filled a box with precious memories. It was eerily quiet in this room; she felt cold and anxious to not remain there a moment longer; she was on her own.

Michael entered the house and started to pour petrol onto the floor and splash it over the walls. "Where's Sarah?" he asked without a second glance, now splashing the container's contents on the carpeted stairs.

"She's right behind us, mate," answered Paul as he hurried out with another box.

Michael was in a nonsensical rage; even he wasn't entirely sure of his actions. But in a way it made perfect sense, and a group fatigued by hauntings and lack of sleep weren't going to stand in his way. Besides, the property wasn't theirs to worry about. His thoughts were muddled and fatigued, yes, but he was aware enough to recognise that his mental state was now breaking down. He'd had enough of the situation and his control had gone. This was the only way in his current state to regain some sense of being in charge.

Sarah found her brother on the stairs. "Michael, wait! You can't just burn down our home!" she pleaded.

Michael responded with a frantic look in his eyes. "Do you have a better idea? Eh? What else are we going to do? Stuff it all, sis." He put the can down and grasped his sister by the shoulder in an attempt to reassure her. "I'll look after you, I've more than enough money." He looked around, wild-eyed. "We're never going to have this place now, they've won!"

Sarah understood. The old house hadn't felt like home for some time, and if she was being honest with herself she too just wanted to be gone. She gave his hand a squeeze and went to join the others, helping them load as much of their equipment as they could get their hands on in time.

Through the house Michael went, ever more rushed, ever more frantic. He put down as much of the petrol as he could, hoping the little he had would do the job. He saved the largest amount for the sturdy front doors, in an almost symbolic gesture. Once done he went back through the hall and out to the shed.

Jane and Paul were at the side door of the van when they heard the Defender come roaring round the corner. "What the bloody hell is he up to now?" Paul asked.

Michael stopped by the gates, blocking the entrance. He knew what he was doing. It was to slow any would be rescue attempt to put the fire out. He was intent that the house must burn and be utterly destroyed. This was the only way.

Julia and Philip were gathering the last of their equipment. Michael, once he was certain everyone was out, went back inside and made his way upstairs. The smell of petrol was overwhelming, but so too were his thoughts. He was after all about to destroy his family home. What was he doing? How could he push his actions on his sister? He continued to head towards the top of the house, his father's Zippo lighter in his hand. He was ready. But before he ignited the flames he stopped, for a moment uncertain whether to now commit to burning down this house, their family home – and home to God knows what was left in here. But what if his actions were to set them free? Could that even be a good thing?

So in the end Michael didn't set the house alight, at least not by his own intention. As he paused, the entity made its last appearance in that grand old house. So startled was Michael he dropped the lighter in mid-reverie. The trail he'd created instantly caught alight and the entity was engulfed in a circle of flame as the fire took hold. He moved back out of the corridor and stood quite still on the very top landing, one hand on the banister, staring at the naked flames licking the walls, tracing the route of the poured petrol. The flames swirled in all directions. Devouring the source of ignition. Michael could feel the heat as it rose so intensely and quickly around him. The fire quickly took hold and began eating its way through the house. Michael made haste before he was consumed as well. He ran down the stairs and into the kitchen and turned on the gas before making his retreat.

When he turned to look, the house was already well on its way to oblivion. He quickly moved the Defender so that the other vehicles could be driven to safety on the other side of the gate. Then the whole group stood watching, in silence but with conflicted thoughts. This beautiful building that had seen so much was succumbing to the inevitable. The corridors, like a smoker's lungs, were filled with smoke, choking the building to death. The spirits were within, moving through the flames, aware of their reality. The ceiling at the very top shattered as it burnt through, cascading its remnants to the floor below. The grand staircase began to groan. A huge supporting roof beam slipped from its housing and came crashing down, bringing with it that section of the roof. There was a sound like thunder as it fell through the floor and the flames rushed into the ground floor, igniting the gas. A quite fantastic explosion erupted, blowing the side wall to pieces and disintegrating the kitchen window. The force of the blast lifted the staircase breaking its back. The furniture was rapidly turning to cinders, leaving nothing for the sprits to play with. The smoke rushed down the tunnel to the crypt, so that smoke could be seen escaping from the ground in the wooded area.

The flames rose higher. The smoke was now billowing into the new day. A silent, mutual decision was made that they had seen enough. Michael positioned the Defender back across the entrance. Andrea seemed to be coming to, but could scarcely be considered awake. No one said a word as they departed. Leaving Michael and Sarah to watch the burning before they too left after mentally saying their goodbyes. They would tell the authorities they were nowhere near the building when it happened.

The house looked as though it was about to cry as the last of the windows blew out from the intensity of the fire, which now had consumed the entire building, the now smoke-filled crypt was acting like a chimney in the woods. The back wall of the house finally gave way and the entire rear of the structure collapsed, spilling itself in a mighty explosion of bricks, wood and burnt debris as it hit the floor and tumbled onto the outbuildings. The fire continued unabated.

As it happened, no one called for the emergency service, no one in the village knew. So the fire was left to complete its work. By the time it had finished the house was no more. There was nothing left but a few charred remains and rubble everywhere. Only the footprint remained underneath it all. The air was filled with the smell of the downfall. It was a sad sight to behold. The once beautiful house was no more.

CHAPTER SIXTEEN

"Hello, Michael." The unmistakably ebullient tone of Peter's voice

It was almost one year to the day of the fire and after an initial stand-off the group had kept in touch. Peter knew Michael and Sarah were returning to the house, though not for the first time. They first had to return for the investigation into the fire. It was put down to malicious circumstances and if any suspicions lay with them they were quickly dismissed. But they hadn't returned since then. They had busied themselves with organising their priorities.

It had been a blessed moment when Michael returned home. Early the next day he called in on Mary; it had seemed to be an age since he'd seen his old companion Flint. He had come wiggling his way to the front door, nearly losing his fluffy dog bum in the excitement of realising his master was home at last. It was the best night any of them had enjoyed in a long time. Safe in Michael's home they sat around the open fire. Flint was a very content little man. The proof was in his snoring. It was a nice memory to add to all the other memories of their companionship, for six months later Flint had passed away from his old age. He left a hole in Michael that never healed. He was truly devastated by the loss of his friend. But his heart was made a little lighter by the company of his sister, who decided to stay for the time being.

Peter had made the phone call as he was keen to return with them to the site of the house. Andrea had regained consciousness, but a week later she had suddenly died. No normal cause was known but they all knew that night had everything to do with it, and Peter was now looking for some kind of closure; to heal the grief for a lost friend. Michael understood all too well. The others were informed but they'd wanted nothing more to do with it.

There was no longer the imposing structure to welcome them when they pulled into the drive, which was pockmarked with overgrown weeds and grass. It was a sorry sight. What was there to greet them was a cement lorry. Michael led the way and ordered the slurry to be poured down the steps. The driver did what the customer asked, not asking or having any idea what it was he was filling in.

Once the truck had left they gathered together. Sarah put flowers down in a sentimental gesture. Not just for them but for the memories, and for the families that had lived there before. She hoped that somehow they were all free now, even the dark entity. The land was sold.

Weeks passed and Michael isolated himself. Only his sister was allowed into his world, but even then at a distance. Friends were discounted entirely. He had no need to engage in any work activity.

One early morning he returned to his favourite place, where he would go when his mind became so muddled and dark. It was raining again. He was on the edge of the cliff looking out to the sea that gave him such peace. He liked writing, handwritten notes were best, he liked the crisp paper when he folded it. For a few seconds he was free, the pain was gone.

Years passed and a new house had been built on the site. A mother was tucking her child into bed.

"Mummy, I saw someone in my bedroom last night."

"There, there, darling it was just a dream."

Printed in Dunstable, United Kingdom